About the Author

Arianne Richmonde is an American writer and artist who was raised in Europe. She lives in France with her husband and coterie of animals. *Shards of Glass* is based on much of her personal experience—she used to be an actress.

As well as **The Pearl Series,** she has written *The Star Trilogy*, and the *USA TODAY* bestselling suspense story, *Stolen Grace*.

Shards of Glass

(The Glass Trilogy #1)

by

ARIANNE

RICHMONDE

This book is a work of fiction. Names, places, characters, and incidents are either a product of the author's imagination or are used fictitiously, not factually. Any resemblance to actual events, locales or persons, living or dead, is entirely coincidental.

Cover design © DonDesigns
Formatting by: BB eBooks

About Shards of Glass

Shards of Glass started out as a very short story I wrote in 2012, with an unexpected twist at the end. I received hundreds of emails and Facebook messages begging me to continue the story and make this into a series. Finally, here it is. Thank you so much for waiting.

Extra thanks to my special friends and team. In no particular order: Sam, Letty, Nelle, Cindy, Dee, Cheryl, Paula, Gloria, Kim, Lisa, Angie, Rachel, Sharon, Tracey, Tracy, Lauren, Marci, Noemi, Patty, Fanci, Siv, Bella, Lilah, Nade, Kathleen, Amanda, Wanda, Jackie, my special Angels, my fabulous Pearlettes, and all the readers and bloggers who have spread the word about my books and added me to your bookshelf.

And last but not least, the two invaluable men in my life: my formatter, Paul Salvette, who has been with me from the beginning and has never let me down, and my husband for his amazing covers.

I'M ALONE IN THE DARK, locked up, with nobody to hear my cries. They've taken him from me. Nobody believes me. She is a liar, a thief, and a fraudster, and probably a murderess. She'll kill him for sure.

Not only does she want me out of the picture . . .

She wants me dead.

PROLOGUE.

THE MINUTE I LAID eyes on him I knew he was dangerous. Why, I wasn't sure, but I also sensed I needed him in some unfathomable way. I, just like everyone else in the company, was in awe of him.

It's a great thing when you know you're going to see the person you're crazy about, every single day of the week. Except Sundays – the day we had off. During rehearsals, that is. Once a show is up and running, though, you perform Sundays.

Then there are the "dark" days: Mondays. Dark, because the theater is empty – no performances. Dark for me because I knew I wouldn't see him.

We were well into week three. Every day I was a bundle of nerves because I knew how lucky I was to have the job. It had been drummed into us at drama school that acting was a thankless career, that only a few lucky percent "make it" and to expect to be either unemployed or learn to love the second string to your bow, because that second string would become your lifeline – your bread and butter. And forget about being a movie or TV star, or even less likely, a Broadway success story – you'd be lucky to get a commercial, lucky to do regional theater. Lucky to get any job at all.

I'm not sure why Daniel Glass picked me for the role. A friend of mine, who also went up for the part—way more beautiful than I consider myself—lost out to me. Her agent told her they said she was "too sophisticated" that they were looking for "somebody with simplicity yet with integral strength." What the hell that meant, I wasn't sure. Trying to get inside the minds of directors and producers is an enigma to me. All you can do is be yourself at the audition and hope for the best, hope your lucky number comes up. That you win the lottery.

Because that is what being an actor is all about. Playing the lottery.

In my mother's day things were even tougher. There was no YouTube, no Internet. They had to send out their 8 x 10s in large manila envelopes via snail mail. Knowing that nine times out of ten, their expensive black and white photo with a résumé stapled to the back, would be thrown into some casting director's waste paper basket. It cost her a fortune. Once, she told me, she got chased around the "casting couch". Literally. A big time British director, famous for vigilante movies, called her in one day. She was over the moon with excitement. She finally had gotten her break, she thought. She was dating my dad at the time, a penniless guitarist back then. The director asked her to come to his "office" at his house. But he didn't ask her to read a script, that day; he made her an offer, instead.

"You can spend ninety-five percent of your time with your penniless guitarist, but the rest of the time I want you to accompany me to premieres, to play my girlfriend—be on my arm," he told her.

She laughed and asked him if he was kidding. Then she found herself running circles around the casting couch while he chased her. When he realized she was serious and it was a definite "no", Mom told me that he turned aggressive and shoved her out of the front door, his gold medallion swinging on his hairy chest. As if the medallion had a life of its own. Shunned. Pride hurt.

I wish my mother were here now to guide me, to give me a hug when I break down from the pressure of wanting to be perfect. Nobody understands that actors are the most insecure human beings alive. Even the stars, even those who are constantly working—even *they* suffer from the fear of being less than wonderful. Actors want to shine, we want to please people and, above all, we want to be loved.

I wanted to please Daniel Glass.

I would have done anything for him.

And I did.

FALL 2012.

"You're late," he says, as I try to slip surreptitiously through the swing doors of the theater, unnoticed.

I pretend I don't hear, and shuffle quietly into a seat at the back. All heads turn, though. All eyes are on me. I lay my satchel gently on the floor.

"I said you're late, Janie," he shouts, his voice booming across the room.

"I'm sorry, I got—"

"Please leave." His voice is still now, cold and deathly, but without anger.

I titter awkwardly.

"Out! I mean it. Out. If you have more urgent things to attend to than rehearsal, I think you'd better attend to them, don't you?"

"I just—"

"I mean it, Janie."

I pick up my satchel and slither out of the room, feeling like a scolded puppy. Daniel hates lateness. He also hates noises that interrupt his train of thought. Or interruption itself. He can't abide that, people chit-chatting in whispers when he's talking. Even if they are discussing what he has just said. No, Daniel wants everyone's undivided attention. Nobody dares avert their eyes. There are certain things he cannot tolerate. However, if you do play by all his rules he is charming. Sweet, even. But if you break a rule . . .

Well, this is the first time it has happened. I'm the first person in the cast to have tested him.

I linger patiently outside. I am the child in the corner. I can hear him talking to the others as I listen to my measured breathing. They are discussing scene two. He wants the character of Jack to wait two more beats before he says his line. Two more beats? Nobody is as precise as Daniel. Would the audience even notice two more beats? Now they're discussing how long a beat actually is. Three seconds? Five? Daniel is telling Jim (who's playing Jack) that he'll feel it instinctively. But I wonder.

Jim, like me, wants to please his director. Even through the thickness of the walls, through the door, I can feel the urgency in Jim's body. He told me the other day that he has never respected a director so much in his life as Daniel, yet he has never worked with a director as young as Daniel, either. Daniel is only thirty. A rising star—the one with the Midas touch. All his productions, so far, have gone to Broadway and toured the major cities of the world. His actors win Tony awards. The pressure is on. We all want to be perfect.

And I was late.

They all begin to file out. Notes are over. Everybody will now spend tonight tossing and turning, questioning Daniel's notes over in their minds.

"Later, Janie," Suzy says, skipping past me.

"Later, Suze."

"Hey Janie, don't take it personally," Frank whispers, as he sidles around me with a grin on his face. Daniel praised him. Told him his kiss with Angela in scene one "spoke volumes". Frank is beaming like the Cheshire Cat.

"See you tomorrow, sweetheart," Angela says, and she strokes me on the cheek. And then she adds in a soft voice, "Don't worry, he'll forgive you."

"See you," I reply dejectedly.

Daniel is still inside the theater. I can hear him shuffling papers. No iPad or tablet, he hates gadgets and only uses his cell in emergencies.

He calls out to me. "Janie? Are you still there?"

I slip through the door quietly.

He isn't looking at me but says, "Stop twiddling your hair, it shows how nervous you are."

How does he know I was twiddling my hair? I was, but how did he *know*? "I'm so sorry I was late."

"You need to get those habits under control," he murmurs, "not good for you, as an actor, to have little traits like that, which can manifest themselves when you're working, when you're supposed to be in character. As an actor, you need to be aware of all your body movements, even the ones you think nobody notices."

He is still looking down at his notes. But then his gaze turns to me, and I feel my insides churn and fold; my heart misses a beat—I sense my shortness of breath. I steady myself against the still half-open door. I feel faint. His eyes are searing into me. Blue. What sort of blue? Prussian blue? They are intense, piercing, rimmed with dark lashes that make perfect sense with his almost black, ruffled hair. But his eyes tell a tale of infinitesimal sadness that gives him a trace of vulnerability. A lie, I think. Daniel is not vulnerable. He's a pillar of strength. My heart is now pounding through my thin pink dress.

"Come here, Janie, I want to talk to you." He motions for me to sit in the chair opposite him, at the small round table, where he has just been giving notes to the others.

I sit down, smoothing my silky dress over my bare knees. Why I chose this dress to wear today, I'm not sure. It's a summer dress, not a Fall dress, but the clear blue sky outside had me fooled this morning. The lyrics to the song, "Autumn in New York" skitter through my mind. There is no place like New York in autumn. There is no place like

New York, anywhere. I love this city.

"You must be freezing in that skimpy outfit," he scolds.

"Not really," I lie.

"It's showing through your bra, just how cold you are," he says, his eyes roving to my pebbled nipples. "Sorry to sound personal, but you really should put on proper clothing. The last thing I need is you getting sick on us all."

My face flushes red, and I realize that I chose this thin little dress to look attractive for Daniel. He *has* noticed me. But in the wrong way.

"Are you eating properly?"

"Excuse me?" I ask. *Who is he? My father?*

"You seem to look faint sometimes. You're so slim, I wonder if you're getting enough nutrition."

"I had a yogurt for lunch and an apple and—"

"Thought so. Not eating enough. Actors need sleep, good food, and plenty of exercise. Stamina. Integral strength—it's part of your job profile. We're still only in rehearsals right now, Janie, but getting out on stage every night, plus matinees, is taxing on the body as well as the brain. You need to look after yourself. Your body is your tool, remember that."

"I go for long walks in Central Park," I venture.

"Not enough." His eyes are looking me up and down, burning through my body, through my almost see-through dress. Can he see my panties? That they are damp? The way he looks at me has made a slick, moist pool gather between my legs. I'd fuck him on the table right here if he asked. But he doesn't see me that way. He sees me as a child. I want to say, *Spank me, then, for being naughty.* I want to say, *Take me across your knee and spank me for being late, for not eating properly, and for being lazy about exercise,* but I answer, "I've joined that gym around the corner from the theater."

"Joining a gym means nothing unless you actually use it. How long ago since you left Juilliard?"

"I graduated this summer."

"That's right, you were one of their little stars." The way he says this doesn't sound like a compliment but a reproach. He raises a cool eyebrow. "So you're even younger than you should be."

"For the role?" A freight train is now racing through my body. Jesus, he's going to fire me! That's why he wanted to talk. I feel my eyes well up.

"So how old are you? Twenty-one?"

My mouth is dry but I manage to croak out a "Yes."

"So young, so vulnerable, so f—"

Daniel is biting his lower lip as his teeth are folded over in an F, but then he stops himself. Am I imagining things? Was he about to say, '*so fuckable?*

"So fearful," he says with a gentle smile. "I'm not going to eat you, Janie. You have tears in your eyes, what's up?"

"Have you brought me here to fire me?"

He laughs. His wide smile lights up his handsome face, his teeth flash white, his eyes crease with mirth. "Is that what you thought?"

But I'm not smiling back. I'm still shivering with trepidation. I cross my legs. The dampness between them really might be showing through my dress. How embarrassing.

"No, Janie. Of course I'm not going to fire you. I'm extremely happy with your work, as it happens."

I want to fling my arms around him. I want to straddle him, sit on his lap. I manage to curve up my lips a little.

"You're making leaps and bounds in rehearsal. You have just the right balance of vulnerability and rawness; it's working beautifully. No, I want to ask you to come with me to the theater tonight. I've been given comps to a play I'd like you to see."

My stomach gives another lurch. *Is Daniel Glass asking me on a date?*

"Do you have a boyfriend?" he asks.

My fantasies are coming true! He wants to date me! "No," I reply, and I notice his eyes flick down to my breasts. I feel myself tingle between my legs again.

"Just asking, in case you wanted to bring him along. In fact, bring a girlfriend, if you want, or your mom."

"My mother's—" I want to say 'dead', but I stop myself. "It's okay, I don't need to bring anyone else." My heart has sunk like a defeated battle ship. He doesn't see me in the date type of way at all.

"I just want you to see Natasha Jürgen play this part. She brings so much vulnerability to her role, but at the end of the play she shows such strength . . . well, I won't say more because I don't want to spoil it for you, but it's important for you,

I think . . . for you to see this play."

"I've heard about it, but I didn't think it had opened yet."

"It's press night tonight. Will you come with me?"

"Are you kidding? I love Natasha Jürgen's work."

"I'll pick you up at seven."

"My address is—"

"I know your address. I'd prefer to come and collect you, that way I can be sure you won't show up late."

"You know where I live?" I ask, butterflies circling my insides like a spring storm.

"You are my employee, I have details about *all* the cast. See you at seven, Janie. Go home, get something to eat and have a nap. You look a little tired."

My eyes linger on his worked-out torso, which I see rippling through his T-shirt, his muscles flexing as he picks up his papers and puts them into a briefcase. *He knows where I live!* The thought of it sends a shiver up my spine. *He's picking me up at my apartment!*

His voice is husky when he says quietly, "See

you later, Janie. Remember, get some rest."

MY TINY STUDIO is my untidy but perfect nest. It's full of clothes and full of plays. I cannot read novels of any kind or guilt sets in. Just plays. Tennessee Williams, Clifford Odets, Shakespeare, Jean-Paul Sartre, David Mamet . . . you name it, I've read them all.

I take off my dress and get into the shower, watching my reflection steam up. I wash my long, chestnut-brown hair and dump half a bottle of conditioner on my fingers, threading them through the tangles, running my fingers through the knots. I look at my face. So little, my body so tiny. I feel like a bird. It's true, I need to eat more. Stop snacking and give myself proper, nutritious meals. My eyes look unusually large and puppy-dog brown, perhaps because I have lost all this weight. Is my part getting to me? I have never felt so vulnerable, never so submissive to a role. I feel as if I have a hole in my heart and the only person that can fill that hole is him. I ache for Daniel Glass. Finally, finally, I have a chance. *He has asked me out!*

I get out of the shower, rub some aromatherapy oil on my wet skin and massage my legs. When I reach my thighs I see Daniel in my mind's eye and imagine his abs pressed against me. The tingle in my groin reminds me I need to release myself—it's been too long. The weeks of torture as I see him in rehearsal every day; the temptation as I watch him work, listen to him direct me in his cool, sexy voice. My instructor. My master. I can't hold it in any longer.

I rummage in my bathroom drawer and reach around for my little "rabbit" and turn it on. I haven't used it for a long while and never would have thought of buying one, but I won it at a friend's bachelorette party. Its rumbling vibration has already got me feeling ready. I'm wet again. Every day I'm that way. Every day, seeing Daniel, hearing him boss me, tell me what to do and command me as my director has me turned on like a switch. I am his submissive. I am his slave. Even though it's my job to do what he tells me, and even though he is kind, I'm still his puppet—his marionette dancing to his tune.

I bring the rabbit in between my thighs and place it on my clit. Aah, oh wow, this feels sexy. It's making me quiver. I rub it around in different places, behind me, now, at the back of my entrance, and then up around the front again. Oh yes, I see Daniel's huge erection, at least how I imagine him: hard as a rock. He's fucking me now. From behind. Oh yes. I let the rabbit enter inside my slick opening and ram it up me as if it were Daniel, then bring it out again, letting it vibrate about my clit. I turn up the power. It's almost thumping me, and I feel the blood rushing inside me, and spasms make my entire body tremble. I lean against the wall. I've reached a climax but I still don't feel satisfied. I need flesh and blood.

I need Daniel himself.

I collapse on my bed, hair still wet, and close my eyes. I think of how he likes me vulnerable, weak, yet he says I must look after myself and be integrally strong. What a paradox. How am I supposed to do that? I stretch out and doze off.

I hear my cellphone go. It feels as if I've been napping for five minutes, but I see that it's five-thirty. I pick up, my head groggy. "Yes?"

"It's Daniel."

"What?"

His voice is almost a growl. "Daniel Glass."

"I know who you are," I say with a giggle.

"Are you going to let me in? I'm outside your door."

"How did you know the elevator code? How did you get through the main door?"

"A neighbor let me up. The one who lives on the fifth floor."

"You're early," I complain.

"Just let me in, Janie. There are some things I need to discuss with you." His voice is commanding, urgent. Am I nuts? This is my wildest fantasy! Why am I procrastinating? I jump out of bed and straighten myself up in the mirror. My smudged makeup is dark around my eyes but it does look a little sexy. Too late, anyway, there's no time. I grab my silky Victoria's Secret robe and go to answer the door.

He's standing there. His jeans are the way they always are. A bit loose but showing off his strong legs, his cute, tight ass. He's a little unshaven, Funny, I didn't notice that earlier. How can a five o'clock shadow spring up that fast?

"Bad girl," he says, moving towards me, into my apartment. He shakes his head. "Bad, bad girl."

"What did I do this time?" I ask nervously.

"Sleeping with wet hair. You'll catch a cold.

Did your mother never warn you against that?"

"She . . . she . . ."

"I'm going to have to punish you for that, Janie, you know that, don't you?"

"Punish me?"

"You need to learn to look after yourself. You need to learn a lesson. Aren't you going to invite me in?"

"But I'm not dressed, I—"

"Your nipples are hard again. I can see them through that skimpy blue robe you're wearing. Is it because you're cold that your nipples get hard all the time or is it because of me?"

"I can't believe you said that, I can't believe—"

"Believe it, Janie. I'm here, aren't I? I came over, didn't I?" His body is close to me now. I can feel his breath on mine, sweet, slightly heavy. His eyes are undressing me. *Oh God, help me, my knees are buckling beneath my feet.*

"I'm going to have to spank you and then—"

My lips part and I want to say something—to protest—but I hear a faint moan emanate from within me. He looks about the room and settles his eyes on my bookshelf.

"David Mamet?" he asks with disbelief. "Steven Berkoff, Tracy *Letts*?"

"My favorite playwrights."

"You like rough, crude characters then, Janie? Like a little aggression, do you, fucked-up, tough-guy characters, tortured souls?"

"Tortured souls have always fascinated me."

"And you think I'm tortured?"

"I don't know, you could be . . . I guess," I splutter.

He takes the paperback, *Speed the Plow,* from the shelf and examines its cover. "She was a little bitch, this character. Unusual for David to write a female role. His wife played the part, did you know that?" Daniel sits on the edge of my bed, with the book in his tight grasp. "Come here." He taps his knees.

I walk over to his side. He gently pulls off my robe and I stand there naked. His large hands cup my butt. "Always been an ass guy, myself. Love your perky tits but it's that ass that gets me going."

He strokes my behind softly. I hear myself moan again. My nipples are like bullets. Suddenly, he bends me over his knee like a child. My eyes are now on the floor, my ass doubled over his strong thighs, which I feel beneath me. My fingers cling to the fabric of his jeans. He's making circular motions with his hands around my butt, and his finger brushes past my opening.

"So wet, Janie. So fucking sexy. You make me rock hard. I don't know if I can stop myself fucking you. My cock's throbbing, can you feel it? Throbbing beneath your tits. It wants to ram itself inside that tight little pussy of yours." His finger is stroking my entrance now. I'm soaking. I can hear soft yielding noises coming from inside me as Daniel runs his finger along my pussy.

"Get ready, Janie – brace yourself."

I feel the paperback slap my behind. Not too hard, but it does sting. Then he softly strokes the lips down there and slips his finger inside me. The smooth with the rough. All I can think about is Daniel ramming his erection into me. Hard.

"Ready, you naughty little girl who doesn't feed herself properly and who goes to bed with wet hair. One, two . . ."

I tense as the book slaps down on my butt again, this time harder. I cry out.

"Again?"

"Yes," I moan. This is so erotic.

He whacks me once more, and this time it

hurts. "Enough?" he asks me.

"More," I murmur, wanting to be brave.

"No. You've been punished enough. I need to kiss it all better now." He cocks up my leg. Turns me around so I am no longer sidesaddle, so to speak, but straddling him with my face down, still looking at the floor, but my thighs splayed on either side of his legs. My butt is high in the air and he lifts it up to his face.

"Got to lick this tight little pussy," he says in a low voice, and his tongue starts to slowly, deliberately circle my clit.

I'm groaning and crying out with pleasure as it flicks about me, teasing me, darting its way in and out, and I begin to writhe with bliss. His thumbs are splaying my lips open as his mouth is sucking, then blowing between my legs. Softly. I'm throbbing and pulsating—the feeling is incredible. Then he lies back on the bed and pulls me right on top of his face.

"Unbutton my jeans," he commands, and I fumble desperately around his crotch, frantically unbuttoning his fly opening. I feel his hard bulge and it makes me gasp. He swirls his tongue around my clit again and I hear myself meow like a cat.

"Push yourself up on all fours," he directs, and I maneuver myself above him. I'm pulling his pants down to his knees, and open up his boxer briefs without taking them off. I free his erection through the soft combed-cotton and take him in my mouth, rimming my tongue around the soft head of his crown.

"I always loved the number 69," he says with a laugh.

I run my lips along his smooth length, kissing as I go. I have only ever done this once before. But it was different then. This time I have Daniel Glass on the tip of my tongue. And like glass, it can be dangerous—it scares me.

"You're so big," I breathe.

He spins me around again by my waist as if I'm a doll, and I'm now on top of him, facing him, my lips on his lips. He has me staring into his eyes. "I want you to ride me," he demands. "Ride me hard. I want you to come around me until your delicate little body can't stand it anymore."

He presses his hand into his jeans' pocket and pulls out a condom packet. "Put this on me, Janie."

"I don't really know how," I reply.

"Please don't tell me you've never done this before. You're not a virgin, are you?"

"Of course not, I'm twenty-one," I protest.

"Well you never know," he says with a crooked grin. "You could be religious . . . or something."

"I don't think you'll find many virgins over the age of eighteen," I say, as if I've had all the experience in the world. The truth is, I have only ever had sex with one boy, and that ended a year ago. But I don't want Daniel to know that. I want him to think of me as worldly.

He pushes me off him. "Come to think of it, you're too young, Janie," he mumbles. "What was I even thinking?" But the mumble is to himself. He kisses me softly but then says, "No, Janie, no, I can't do this to you. You're too young. Too vulnerable."

Hot. Cold. I can't stand the torture.

He's killing me softly with this kiss, *Killing Me Softly* with his words, the tune swims in my mind— all I want is him. All I desire is Daniel Glass inside me, even if that glass cuts. Even if it wounds me.

"Please," I beg. "Please. I need you. You're my director. In every way. I'm so crazy about you, it hurts. I come to work every day obsessing about you, desiring you in every movement I make, every step I take. Everything I do is for you, Daniel."

"Don't."

"Don't what? Tell you that you're a god to me? That even if you hurt me sometimes, I love you anyway? That I can't get you out of my mind? Nor night nor day. I love you, Daniel Glass. I love you."

"Let's just lie side by side and hold each other, Janie darling."

He called me darling. I'm in a swoon.

"Be still, Janie."

He kicks off his jeans and pulls them, and his boxer briefs, away from his toes until we are lying naked, side by side. His body is beautiful. Worked-out but not overdone. Smooth like caramel, faintly tanned but not too bronzed. His lips are curved, the corners lifting upwards as if somebody is pulling invisible threads. His skin is clear and unblemished, his nose straight with the tiniest bump that makes him look like a Greek statue. He tells me I'm too young for him, yet I feel his hardness pressed up against my skin. I let my hands wander south and feel him there. He groans. He doesn't push my hands away.

"I love you, Daniel," I say again, and every cadence in my voice speaks the truth. I would die for this man.

"I love you, too, my little Juilliard star. You're precious to me. You shine like a diamond, half cut, half polished. You're special, but not everyone has seen how bright you'll shine. But they will. I'm going to pull that out of you. Coax it out. I'm going to make you weak, yet strong."

"How?"

"By making love to you. I'm going to have to fuck you, Janie." He pulls me close to him and I slip on his huge erection with ease, my wetness surrounding him like a knife cutting into oozing butter.

He starts making small thrusts as we lie side by side and he kisses me, his tongue darting into my open mouth, greedily sucking me, licking me. It feels ... ooh, so ... so good. I claw onto his muscular ass with my nails, leveraging my body to ease myself up and down him. I want him in ... deep.

"You, Feel. So. Good. I. Love. Fucking. You," he growls, plunging his way in harder. He's above me and has my ass in his hands, lifting my buttocks up with each thrust. He's controlling me, dominating me, totally fucking me. In out, in, out. Aah, it feels incredible, all my nerves are on fire. I'm soaking wet. I'm like this tiny thing and his huge hard cock is taking over my body. Whole. Each time he slams it in, he pulls me tight towards his groin. We are one, our hips meeting as close as is physically possible.

"I love you, Daniel."

"Sweet little tight pussy," he says groaning. "Making. Me. So. Fucking. Hard!" Each thrust is punctuated by a word. His voice is raw. I have this powerful man weak with desire and I feel hot. He rolls me over in one sudden pull so I'm now on top of him. His erection has slipped out with the movement so I guide it back in with my two hands. The pressure of his cock slapping against my clitoris has me screaming with pleasure and, as I push it inside me, I feel myself coming—the rush and spasms making me climax in two places, my clit and deep down within me. My tits are smacking his chest, my nipples rosy and firm, my nerve-endings electric.

"That's right, baby, come hard, come around my cock, oh yes."

His tongue is inside my mouth, exploring every last bit of me, his eyes intense as he cries out. I feel his erection thicken and stiffen even more. My body trembles and quivers as he explodes inside of me. "I'm coming Janie, I'm coming hard."

His mouth is on mine, tongues wrapped about each other, orgasms uniting in one golden shimmering firework.

I hear my cell ring. *What the—*

I bolt up with a jerk. My hands are pressed between my legs. Now I know the meaning of a wet dream. There's sweat all over me. My bed is empty. Daniel Glass is nowhere to be seen. I grab my cellphone and look at the time. 6.55 p.m. Holy smoke! I can still feel the tingles pushing through me, my post-orgasmic body shot with a thunderous bolt. I press ANSWER.

"I'm outside your apartment building." It's Daniel. His voice is clipped. Urgent.

"I'll be down in a second."

"Don't be long," he warns. "I don't want us to be late. Curtains go up at eight sharp. I'd hate to let my fiancée down."

His words are groggy syllables in my head. "Your f . . . fiancée?" I stammer.

"Yes, didn't you know? Natasha Jürgen is my fiancée. We're getting married in two weeks. Don't want to be late for her greatest performance yet."

His sentence cuts through me like splintering shards of glass.

He adds, "You need to see Natasha act; you could learn a lot from her. Now get your heinie down here, Miss Janie Juilliard. Right now, or we'll be late."

"Coming," I blurt out, realizing the irony of what I just said.

1

OBSESSION IS A DANGEROUS THING. You can call it infatuation, or even love, you can call it whatever you like, but it is a sickness. Even Shakespeare knew that. Especially Shakespeare. Daniel was my every thought, my every movement. He consumed me. He eked his way into my nightly dreams, where we would be in love. Not unrequited love, but tangible and equal—both of us crazy for each other, simultaneously. Then I'd wake up empty. This happened every night. Over and over again.

That evening, when he took me to the theater, when I watched Natasha Jürgen's performance in awe—and envy—was humiliating. A slap in the face. They were going to get married. He was in love with her: a glamorous, worldly, thirty-five-year-old. I was out of her league. She had long blond hair, breasts that any woman would kill for. She was a beautiful, Teutonic force of power, with legs that went on forever, and a bewitching smile. She commanded the stage. I wept at her performance, sad tears, happy tears. I was bowled over. It felt that it was the most catalytic moment of my life, because observing her made me more determined than ever to hone my craft; become the actress I knew I was born to be. Little did I know that a far more life-changing moment was yet to come.

In the months that followed, however hard I tried, I couldn't rid myself of Daniel, neither physically nor mentally. I was working with him—seeing him nearly every day in rehearsals, and when we were done rehearsing, we would be performing by night; his eyes on us. His ears. Afterwards he'd give us notes backstage. Even when we'd been up and running for a month, Daniel was still there in the wings, up in the gods, front row sometimes—you never knew. But he'd be studying our every move. A tilt of the head, a twitch of a smile; nothing went unnoticed with

Daniel. He was a perfectionist.

I would often click on Wiki and read the official Daniel Glass bio. Like a glutton for punishment, I needed to remind myself whom I was dealing with. A man out of my league. Worse: a *married* man. A man who could never be mine.

Daniel James Glass is an American stage director. He was born in New York City, the only child of Valerie Peterson, a university English professor, and Wilson James Glass, a self-made billionaire who amassed his fortune by way of the auto parts industry. His father, who was from New Hampshire, was of Scottish and Italian descent.

Glass' parents divorced when he was a child. He grew up in Manhattan and attended Yale and later Magdalen, Cambridge University, England, where he graduated with a double first in English (summa cum laude). While at Cambridge, he was a member of the Marlow Society and acted in, and directed, several plays, including a production of David Mamet's *Speed The Plow*, which got him noticed by Harold Pinter, who cast him to play Albert Stokes in *A Night Out* at the National for which he won the Laurence Olivier Award in 2005. According to Pinter, as well as being "an outstanding actor" Glass was also a "brilliant" cricketer, and played for Magdalen College.

In 2012 he inherited his father's vast fortune, after Wilson Glass died of pancreatic cancer. In that same year, Glass married the actress Natasha Jürgen.

I needed to read that last line. Needed to drum it into my head.

I repeated to myself, over and over like a mantra, "He's married, Janie. Worse, he's in love—not even in your dreams, Janie. Not even in your dreams."

Yet, however much I tried, I could not squash those dreams and wayward fantasies. Daniel Glass was my world. I breathed for *him* more than for myself.

My hard work and obsession with pleasing him did pay off though. Seven months later, I was nominated for a Tony award. I didn't win, nor did I expect to. I lost out to the invincible Natasha Jürgen. Lost out in every way. She had it all. The man. The beauty. The talent. The glittering career.

And then, one day, she didn't.

Just like that, it was all over.

2

I HEARD THE NEWS six months after we finished the play. I was at my parents' house in Vermont. Well, Mom had been dead for several years, but I still referred to it as my parents' house. I was at the pottery wheel, throwing a bowl, and when the news came on the radio, my suddenly unsteady hands caused the clay to flop all over the place and spin off the wheel in an oozy mess. My late mother was a professional potter, and my dad was a carpenter; both having given up acting and music to pursue other interests—those that could actually pay the bills. He still kept the workshop and business, where he sold their one-of-a-kind, custom-made artwork which, after years of hard work, had now become quite profitable. I was spending time with him and my younger brother, Will, at our house near Stowe for a few weeks, until I started a new job in New York: a guest role on a TV show.

A female voice interrupted the music I was listening to on the radio: Brahms, I think it was.

"The Tony award-winning Broadway actress, Natasha Jürgen, has tragically and unexpectedly died. She passed away in the early hours of this morning, at Lennox Hill Hospital, New York City, where she had been admitted after an accident with a swerving bicycle while she was crossing the road in Central Park, yesterday. Apparently, the actress seemed uninjured even though she had bumped her head in the fall. Witnesses say she got up and laughed about it, refusing to be admitted to the hospital, after an ambulance had arrived at the scene. However, a few hours later, she complained of a headache, and her husband, director Daniel Glass, insisted he take her to the hospital. She fell into a coma last night. The cause of death was an epidural hematoma. The family thanks everyone for their kind condolences and ask for privacy at this very sad time. A funeral will be held later this week in an undisclosed location."

You would have thought I would have been . . . how can I put this . . . secretly hopeful . . . wishful that Daniel would choose me to fill his unhappy void, to be his shoulder to cry on, be his special friend. That one day he could love me the way he loved his wife. But, no. I was *horrified* by her death. Sickened. Literally. A nauseous wave of bile rose in my throat, and the pottery wheel spun around, my hands, thick and withered with wet clay, which was embedded also in my fingernails. I got up and stumbled over to the washbasin, shoving my hands under the flowing tap, and I vomited as if all my insides would spill out.

I hated myself.

I really did.

Because only a few days before I had let my mind wander again to my Daniel fantasies, wishing that something would happen to make them split up, that she would turn out to be a raving lesbian and not want Daniel, and that he would turn to me for comfort, fall madly in love with me and forget all about her. Or, that she'd get snapped up by Leonardo di Caprio and that Daniel would decide that Natasha had been wrong for him all along. Many scenarios had passed through my mind, but *death?* That, I had never imagined, not even in my wildest fantasies. No way. But I had obviously jinxed her. I had killed Natasha Jürgen, *unwittingly*, with the power of my wishful thoughts.

Knowing this made me to never, ever, want anything to do with Daniel again.

3

"THE PRODUCERS ARE GOING to love you," my friend Star cajoled, in her domineering 'I-know-what's-best-for-you' voice. "The role is made for you."

Her beautiful face was on my iMac screen—we were on Facetime. She flicked back her long blond hair and widened her almond-shaped blue eyes at me, not wanting to take no for an answer. Star was a star. Not just *any* star but a mega-movie star commanding thirty million a picture. She was married to Jake Wild, the sexy British director who, like Star, had recently won an Oscar. The two gave Brangelina a run for their money; glamorous, loaded, philanthropic (all her elephant saving and school foundations in third world countries), and they were serious eye-candy, the pair of them.

"They don't want little old me," I told her. "They'll want a real *movie* star, someone who's got lots of film experience. All I've done is theater and that one guest role on that crappy TV show that I play down and hope will disappear off my resume because I don't want anyone to know about it."

"They *do* want you because I've convinced them. And they listened."

My heart gave a little leap, but I knew better than to get myself all excited. "They're just *pretending* to listen to you, Star, but when the chips are down, they'll pick a name."

"You *are* a name, Janie."

"In the theater, a little. But I'm a nobody in the movie world."

"For now. Believe me, that will change. They want to meet with you the day after tomorrow."

"Here, in New York?"

"No, in LA."

"For an audition?"

"They don't need to audition you, they saw your Tony nominated performance. They know you can act."

"Who's 'they?' "

"Surprise. I won't tell you or you'll start Googling them and then get all nervous. Best you just walk in there coolly without letting on you give a damn."

"One thing is acting, but what about the role itself? I heard through the grapevine about this part and was told it was for someone sexy. That there are sex scenes and hot—"

"You *are* sexy, Janie, trust me."

I looked at myself on my laptop screen, in the little box. No, not sexy. My unkempt long brown hair and delicate face was interesting, maybe, and attractive, but not overtly sexy. My body was little. Too petite. Small ass. 'B' cup size, at best. And that was on a good day if I wore a padded bra. Hell, half the time I didn't even wear a bra, so I didn't actually know my size for sure. What was the point? There was nothing much to hoist up. I started to bite my lip and twiddled my hair with nerves. Bad habits. I could hear Daniel, in my head, chastising me.

"Anyway," continued Star. "It's all arranged. I'm sending a limo to take you to JFK tomorrow. Be ready and packed by eight a.m. I'll email you your flight details. In fact, I'm sending them right now. First class and—"

"Really Star, you—"

"No arguing. I'll be at LAX to pick you up, and then you're staying with us, at our beach house in Malibu. Gotta go. Wait for instructions. In two seconds this Facetime session will self-destruct," she joked. And she was gone.

I still couldn't believe I was friends with *Star freaking Davis*! She had come backstage after my performance one night at the theater, and insisted on taking me out to dinner afterwards. It was surreal. The paparazzi were there. Johnny Depp, and a bunch of friends of Star's. We all went to Sardi's and she ordered vegan pizza for everybody. Madonna came by to say hello and told me she'd heard my performance was "exquisite." Star and I stayed in touch after that. Strangely, she was in awe of me—fascinated by the theater, but too nervous to give it a go herself. "The stakes are too high," she'd said. I felt honored to have this two-time Oscar winning actress as my friend. She was only a couple of years older than me, and somehow I knew we'd be friends for years to come.

I SLEPT MOST of the plane ride. After the spring chill of New York it felt great to feel the warm LA sun on my back. Star picked me up in her convertible Porsche and, with a large hat and oversized sunglasses, she got away with not being recognized (for all of five minutes) before a curious crowd formed; mothers with their children, young couples, even an old man, demanding autographs. I still couldn't get my head around the fact that she was so famous, having momentarily forgotten, until pandemonium broke loose all around us. But Star seemed in a rush and wasn't interested in signing autographs and making small talk.

She grabbed my suitcase from me and wheeled it behind her, racing ahead of me. "Hubby will kill me for going out without my bodyguard, but hey, I need my independence, you know?"

"Excuse me, excuse me, are you Star Davis?" a woman yelled, trotting after us.

I had to practically sprint to keep up with Star.

"You know," she told me, "when I traveled around the world with a backpack a few years ago, I cut my hair short and dyed it black, and almost nobody recognized me. Good days, although I mustn't complain, being accosted comes with the job." She winked at me. "You'll soon understand. When you get famous, I mean."

I laughed. "Yeah, right. I'm just a working actress, Star. I don't think fame is in the cards for me."

"You'll see. I'm driving you to your meeting by the way."

My stomach dipped. "Not now though. We're stopping by your house first, right?"

"No. No time. Straight to Paramount, to the lot. Sorry, but they brought the meeting forward. No worries, hon, you look great."

"I look like shit," I said, glaring at her. She ignored me as if going to a Hollywood meeting with a group of powerhouse producers was the easiest, breeziest thing in the world. For her, I guess it was. Star had been famous most of her life, had started acting when she was only two years old, won an Oscar at ten, then again for her role in *Skye's The Limit*. She had obviously forgotten what it was like to be a flesh and blood human being, with nerves and insecurities—well, when it came to movies, anyway.

Once we were in the car, she revved up the engine unnervingly, hugging corners and going beyond the speed limit. Our hair was flying in the wind like ragged sails. She was oblivious to my gritted teeth, my hand gripping the sun-warmed seat. Not to mention my anxiety at the thought of meeting three producers who I was sure were doing Star a favor by agreeing to see me. They probably had the part already cast and were just appeasing her. Because if they were serious, they would have called my agent and arranged an official screen test.

Star glanced at me and then set her eyes back to the road. "Dig out that Dolce & Gabbana shopping bag from the back. There's a dress inside I bought for you. To wear to the meeting."

I leaned back and pulled out a bag. "Star, really, let me pay you back. You can't go round buying me expensive outfits."

"You can't go round buying *yourself* expensive outfits, sweetie. Not with your off-Broadway paycheck. Plus, don't you have that student loan still hanging over your head? Anyway, it's not Dolce & Gabbana, it's vintage Halston. And it's beautiful. And more importantly, sexy. Yet classy. I'll pull over in a minute and you can slip it on."

"What, on the side of the road?"

"You're a performer, you're used to quick changes."

I pulled the dress out of the bag and ran my fingers over the soft, black fabric. "1970s?"

"1970 is your era, Janie. Small, perky, pre-pubescent boobs were big back then—I mean 'in' back then, not 'big.' " She laughed at her blunder. "Remember Katharine Ross in *Butch Cassidy and the Sundance Kid? The Graduate? The Stepford Wives?* She was *the* A-list actress. The 'it' girl everybody wanted to be. She was pretty flat chested. Ditto Faye Dunaway, Sissy Spacek, Mia Farrow. That's your look, that's your niche, Janie."

Thanks, Star, for pointing out the flat chested part. I felt ashamed. Not about my small boobs but about my lack of film knowledge. I'd read every play known to man, but my movie repertoire was sketchy. Star was a film buff—not only had she seen everything, but she viewed her life through movies; every reference was a movie—and she was personally acquainted with half the actors that had starred in them too, even the golden oldies like Robert Duvall.

I rummaged about in the bag and pulled out a pair of high, platform shoes. Black. They were my size. "How did you know I'm an eight?" I asked her.

"I learned that trick from my husband. Called the wardrobe department at the Playroom Theater and found out."

I laughed. "Stalker. You could have asked me directly."

"It would have spoiled the surprise." She slowed down somewhat, easing her foot off the accelerator. She was about to tell me something important. "Janie, you've heard of Pearl Chevalier, haven't you? You know she's one of the producers you're meeting today."

"Course I've heard of her. She's only one of the most powerful producers in Hollywood. And her husband, Alexandre Chevalier, is like, the richest man in the world."

"The seventh richest," Star said seriously.

My stomach made a nervous flip again. I was so not looking forward to this meeting; being grilled by big shots and then told "*Don't call us, we'll call you.*" The truth was I was using this trip as a sort of vacation. Hang out with Star. Catch a few rays. Then I'd go back to New York, back to my humble apartment with bad plumbing and noisy neighbors on the Upper West Side, and start auditioning again for plays. Even being nominated for a Tony Award was no golden ticket these days. Acting was hard work. Well, not so much the acting itself, but landing the jobs in the first place. Getting the audition was bad enough, but then doing a great reading, being right for the role, catching the director when he or she hadn't gotten up on the wrong side of bed that day. Having the right sized boobs. Yes, even that. There were so many factors; talent, it seemed, was the least of it. I was already thinking about Plan B in my mind. Waiting tables? But my skills were paltry—even waiting tables was too taxing—the one job I had at a swanky Italian restaurant, I screwed up. Spilled drinks all over some CEO, and another time fell flat on my face with a bunch of plates stacked on my arms. That was the problem; all I'd ever done successfully was act. Or make squiffy pots out of clay. I had so few other skillsets.

Star must have sensed my insecurity. "Take that scrunched eyebrow look off your pretty face, Janie. You'll be fine. Pearl is very friendly and she's on your side."

The words "on your side" gave me a clue as to

where this meeting would be going. Star had obviously bullied Pearl into considering me for the part, and the other producers would be dead against hiring an unknown actress. They were *not* on my side, clearly. I sighed and just decided to take the whole thing as something to check off as "experience." I'd be friendly, professional, and try to be myself. What more could I do? And I'd stick on the Halston vintage dress, and the platforms I probably wouldn't be able to walk in, just to please Star.

I slipped on the little black 70s number and touched up my makeup while we were driving. A hint of gloss and some mascara, nothing more. I never did look good with too much makeup. Before I knew it, we'd arrived at the studio lot. Star handed her car keys to a valet, and we found our way through a labyrinth of hangars, before we arrived in the lobby where we were meant to be. It wasn't sleek and monochrome, or fancy in any way. It was a nondescript beige room with a soda machine and a bored-looking woman behind the reception desk, who barely acknowledged me when Star introduced us. I guessed the woman— who wore a long flowy dress—was used to seeing movie stars and was nonplussed. Very LA.

"I'm just going to use the ladies' room," Star said, and before I had a chance to say, 'me too,' she added, "you wait here, just in case," and she skipped off, leaving me standing there in my rockety, unstable heels.

The shoes were agony so I took them off, and as I was readjusting the straps, trying to figure out which way the buckles were meant to be—front or back—the receptionist said, "They're ready for you now, Miss Cole."

"Star's—"

"If I were you, I'd go straight in. Sam Myers has another appointment to go to, he won't like being kept waiting."

My nervous fingers gave up fumbling with the straps. What was the point, anyway? I knew they weren't going to hire me; shoes or no shoes. "Sure," I answered, my throat dry. I walked towards the door in my bare feet, strappy sandals in hand, knowing the fact the receptionist hadn't even given me a script meant this meeting was bullshit. Not a bona fide audition at all.

I pushed the door open. There was a long conference table and at the helm sat a very fat, oily-looking man: the infamous Samuel Myers. I'd seen his picture on the Internet. He was the producer for that massive blockbuster trilogy with Alessandra Demarr in the lead, the lesbian actress who dated Alexandre Chevalier's sister, Sophie Dumas. *Stone Trooper.* I hadn't seen the movies—they were up to *Stone Trooper 3*, but they were very popular and had made him, and everyone involved, rich. Stinking rich. Even less chance of him hiring a mere theater actress like me for his new project.

"Come in, Janie," he boomed in a paradoxically wheezy voice, because booming and being wheezy at the same time shouldn't have been possible. "Shoes uncomfortable?"

"Shoes a pain in the neck," I shot back, refusing to let him intimidate me. I glanced along the table. Pearl Chevalier was sitting demurely, with her legs crossed, in what looked like a cream-colored Chanel suit. Tan Louboutins, because I caught a glimpse of the scarlet red soles. Her blond hair was in an elegant chignon, and her pearl earrings shone like the polished jewels they were. She instantly got up. I noticed Samuel Myers didn't.

"Janie Cole, congratulations on *Where the Wind*

Blows, you were outstanding," she said, a friendly smile spread across her face.

"You saw it?"

"Of course. It was the talk of New York, I wouldn't have missed it for the world. Sam, you philistine, you missed out on a great performance and a stunning play. Shame on you."

I padded over in my bare feet to shake Pearl Chevalier's hand. Ladies first. I could feel Sam Myers's eyes on my backside. As I turned to shake his hand as well, the door swung open.

"Sorry I'm late," a voice I knew so well said. "Not used to driving. Got caught in traffic."

I could feel myself go faint and I leaned against the table for support. *This* I was not expecting. What the hell was *he* doing here? I spun around.

"Hello, Janie," he said, his signature blue eyes piercing my psyche, unraveling a year's worth of inner determination to let him go, in just one easy glance. I felt the air get sucked out of my lungs— the power he still had over me was alarming. I thought I had gotten over him. Obviously not.

"Hi Daniel," I managed. I sounded cool, because more words escaped me. I should have teased him about arriving late, sent him out of the room, but my brain wasn't working that fast. What else could I have said? I hadn't seen him, nor spoken to him, in forever. The flowers I sent to honor his dead wife felt hypocritical—a lie. But I sent them anyway because it was the decent thing to do. But I hadn't been decent. My thoughts of him never pure. He had controlled me like a puppet. Worse, I had become a feverish madwoman. Obsessed. Possessed by him. Painful, unrequited love that could rival any Shakespeare play. And I never, ever wanted to be in that vulnerable place again.

I turned back to Samuel Myers and said, "So thrilled to meet you, Mr. Myers. Just love the *Stone Trooper* movies."

"You've seen them?" he asked, an eyebrow suspiciously raised. "Wouldn't have thought they were your cup of tea—a true *thespian* like yourself." His tone was sarcastic.

I gave him a sly smile and said no more. Lying was my job. I lied every day. That's what actors do; they lie. They trick people. But he had my number. And I could tell already, he didn't like me.

"Siddown," he commanded, as he managed to pull a chair out for me, still without getting up. "I want to have you close so I can see what all the fuss is about for myself."

I wondered where Star was. She should be here by now. But then it dawned on me . . . her visit to the bathroom was a ruse. Maybe she even knew about Daniel all along.

"Siddown, Daniel," Sam said, "next to our lovely Pearl."

I had my back to Daniel as I sank into a swivel chair. I could sense him behind me and I felt a nauseous wave engulf me once more. *Get a grip, Janie! What is wrong with you?* Was it my imagination or could I feel his breath on my neck?

"I missed you, Janie," he mumbled in my ear. He splayed his fingers lightly on my shoulder as he said it, his thumb brushing my bare flesh. I shivered. I could feel a familiar pulse between my legs. A pulse that he had always inspired. This man could destroy me. And I couldn't let him. I had to stay composed.

Daniel quickly moved away and walked to the opposite side of the table, where he sat beside Pearl. He narrowed his laser-blue eyes, studying me as if I were an object of art. Sizing me up. A commodity. A tool for his next success. I assumed he was going to be the director for this movie and that's what he was doing here. Hell, I still didn't even know what the film was called—not even the working title—nor anything about it. This whole situation was insane. Unorthodox. They would have called my agent if this were for real.

"Well," said Pearl, cutting through the terse atmosphere in her Ivy-league educated voice, "you all know why we are gathered here today."

Gathered here. Made it sound like a funeral. And it was. My funeral. Where I would get buried beneath the complex, powerful character that was Daniel Glass. Where he would mould, and dominate and break me. Make me a whimpering wreck who dreamed about him 24/7. I could feel my core dampen; just thinking about what he could do to me. How hard he could fuck me. How he could make me come a thousand ways if he chose to do so. But he didn't see me that way. No, I was a vessel for his art, not for his lust or love. If he'd had any interest in me he'd had nearly a whole year to get in touch. Invite me for a coffee. A walk in the park. Nothing. And here he was, suddenly appearing out of nowhere. Obviously he needed me. But not in the way that I'd fantasized about.

"Janie, I want you on board for this film," Daniel said in a sharp, unapologetic voice. God I loved that voice. Deep, rumbling. That voice had given me so much pleasure. And pain.

"Why didn't you just call, Daniel?" I threw out, challenging him with an equally sharp look, eye to eye.

"Because the casting is not my final decision, and I didn't want to get your hopes up."

"And what makes you all think I want this job so desperately?" I heard myself say. It was as if another character lived inside me. A confident, brash, superstar, who didn't give a damn. "After all," I continued, "I haven't even been sent a script. How do I know what the writing is like? You haven't even mentioned what part you want me to play, nor anything about the storyline."

"We only confirmed Daniel as the director two days ago," Pearl explained. "And it's true, the whole thing has been very spontaneous and last-minute. Samuel wanted to meet you, Janie. Me too. Daniel has already made it clear you're his first choice for the role."

"Mr. Myers might change his mind when he sees a screen test. Maybe I'm unphotogenic, perhaps I don't have a rapport with the camera the way I do with the audience on stage. I think all this is very precipitous." *Precipitous?* Who *was* this haughty alter ego that was taking me over? I guessed I was doing everything I could to sabotage my chances of being offered the part, whatever the part was. That way, I couldn't be hurt. Star had instructed me to be nonchalant, but this? My attitude was downright negative, even rude. And definitely ungrateful.

Daniel said in an even voice, "We still don't have a script, Janie. That's why we haven't sent you one. This is going to be very ad-lib. Lots of improvisation. You know, I wanted to go in the direction of someone like the British director, Mike Leigh. That's why I need a strong, theatrically trained cast. I'm not going to be doing hundreds of takes a scene. Not my style. You know, I need actors who can sustain one, long, fifteen-minute take—who know how to choreograph their way around a scene, without fucking up, without fluffing their lines."

Samuel glared at Daniel. The F word was obviously not welcome, despite his own uncouth manners.

I turned to the overweight producer. Beads of sweat were gathering on his brow. I said, "Excuse me, Mr. Myers, but isn't this kind of film a little too experimental for the likes of you, whose repertoire is a chain of blockbusters and all-star rom-coms?"

He chortled with a loud snort, his belly jiggling like a greasy chef in a bad restaurant. "Smart girl. She's onto us, Pearl. Haven't you heard of such a thing as 'tax deduction,' Janie?"

Pearl broke in, "Sam, *really*! Janie, this is absolutely *not* why we want to do this film—please don't be offended. This is going to be an *art* movie; we need to lend our bigger projects, and Hooked Up Enterprises, more credibility, *creatively* speaking. I was stunned by your performance, Janie, and I was the one to contact Daniel in the first place. Daniel agreed. An actor of your caliber would do us proud. You could carry this film."

I took in a deep breath. I didn't know whether to feel insulted or flattered. I was about to be Hooked Up Enterprise's tax loss experiment. Samuel Myers told it like it was, and I admired his honesty. Especially in the notoriously bullshitty world that was Hollywood. At least I knew where I stood.

"She's not sexy enough," Samuel suddenly announced, as if I weren't in the room. "Sorry, honey, you know it. I know it. This is a hot-blooded love story we're talking about. A la francais. Close ups in private places. Think *Last Tango in Paris*. Think Sharon Stone crossing and uncrossing her legs."

My alter ego took over again. I could feel my cheeks burning, my veins surging with bubbling blood. How *dare* he tell me that I wasn't sexy! How dare this pig of a man judge me like a book cover.

I got up from my seat and walked over to Daniel. Startled, Daniel looked up at me as I straddled him, my Halston dress rising high as my smooth bare legs gripped either side of his muscular thighs. I sat on his lap facing him and, leaning in close, started to slowly lay my lips on his. Shocked into stillness, he did nothing. Just closed his eyes in resignation, his nearly black hair flipping over his brow. I could smell him. Clean. Rough. Uncompromising. A bullet of sexuality and intensity straight to my fluttering heart. And elsewhere. In that instant, he was all mine. My tongue darted out and I flicked it on his mouth, trailing it seductively along his full lips. They parted, and I heard him take in a sharp breath. I kissed him. Hard. To my amazement I felt his erection strain against his slacks. I continued the kiss, licking, sucking gently, nipping. I groaned quietly—almost imperceptibly—into his mouth, which tasted of oranges and mint. Then, as abruptly as I'd accosted him, I got up.

"There," I said. "Consider *that* my audition." I turned to Pearl and smiled. "Nice meeting you," and I made a B-line for the door.

I could hardly believe what I'd just done. *What had gotten into me?*

Star was waiting outside.

"So?" she said, her eyes wide with expectation, "how did it go?"

"Run," I cried, grabbing her by the wrist. I realized I'd left the sexy shoes behind, but I didn't care—they could keep them as a memento. "We need to get the hell out of here before I get arrested."

4

I RELATED MY OUTRAGEOUS behavior to Star, who was giggling and driving at the same time, the wind whipping her hair across her face.

"It's not funny, Star. Something in me took over."

"What you did was puuuurfect." She slapped her hand on the steering wheel in glee. "You'll see."

"What I'll 'see' will be one hundred percent humiliation. Daniel will never want to set eyes on me again; he must think I'm some kind of horny slut. Pearl Chevalier will no doubt be shocked and wish she'd never called me in, and Samuel Myers, despite not thinking me sexy, will go home and whack off, but will still not want me for the role."

I sighed, and gathered my hair into a ponytail to stop it blowing into my lips. "Besides, I don't want that part anyway. I don't *want* to cross and uncross my legs while the camera takes a close up. I don't *want* to be 'fucking' some lame actor on a high definition screen when I am a respected theater actress. This is not a good move for me professionally."

"I don't know. If it's in the name of art and the shots are cool and interesting and artistic?"

"I doubt they will be if tacky Samuel Myers has anything to do with the creative side of the film."

"That's where Daniel Glass comes in. He'll make sure it looks good."

"There's many a slip 'tween cup and lip."

"That's from *Hamlet*, isn't it?"

I nodded. "I think so. The old bard was wise. Daniel is a very talented theater director but he has little experience with film, and certainly the Hollywood Machine. Anything could go wrong. Even midway in the shoot. He'd be under Sam Myers's porky fat thumb."

Star laughed. "Yeah, I've heard old Sam's pretty slimy, but Pearl seems to have him wrapped around her pinkie finger. She's clever that way;

never antagonistic, but always gets what she wants. Janie, you're no fool and your instincts could be spot on. Shame, I so wanted for you to be part of my world. Never mind, we'll find another leading role for you. I'll call Steven, and I know Sandra has some cool stuff going on."

Steven Spielberg and Sandra Bullock, no doubt. Star knew them all.

"You happy with your agent?" she asked. "You want to meet mine?"

"I'm a loyalist, Star. My agent helped me get *Where the Wind Blows*. I won't change her now, whatever carrot is dangled before me."

"You're a good person, you know that? Decent. In fact you're too good for your own good. That's a lot of 'goods' in one sentence! There aren't many like you in this town."

I shook my head in denial. I *wasn't* a good person. But I didn't want to tell Star why—share the Daniel story with her. My unhealthy obsession with him, resulting in his wife dying, only days after I'd wished ill on them. I wanted to believe it was fate, a coincidence—nothing to do with me, but deep in my bones I knew that wasn't true. Thought is powerful. Admitting to myself I had bad karma coming my way was difficult enough, but letting others in on my secret was harder— nobody else needed to know. Maybe Hollywood, with its lies and deception, would suit me perfectly after all.

STAR AND I STOPPED off for a coffee in Brentwood on the way back to her house. She donned the big hat and shades again, and kept her back to the street—we were sitting outside on a terrace. So far, nobody was bothering her. She checked her messages so I did the same.

I listened to my voicemail.

The first was from Pearl Chevalier. She got straight to the point. "Janie, I have to admit I was pretty shocked by what you did in our meeting . . . "—my stomach turned inside out. I'd embarrassed myself, *and* her. I listened to the rest of the message—"However, it certainly got Sam's attention and he has changed his mind about . . . how should I say this? He has a different opinion now about your assets and talent."

I sniggered to myself. *Talent? Straddling and kissing someone is a talent now, is it?*

Pearl's message continued: "But now there's a

new problem. Daniel Glass and Sam Myers do not see eye to eye on how the movie should be shot, the look and feel of it, specifically concerning the sex scenes. And I'm somewhere in the middle. I'll call again later, meanwhile sit tight."

The next message was from Samuel Myers himself. Before he even opened his mouth I knew it was him, because there was a bout of heavy, wheezy breathing coming down the line. Finally he spoke: "Jane," he said, getting my name wrong," I eat my words. I see who you are now. You are *Rambling Rose*! And I like it. I like it very, very much. I'll be in contact. Don't fly back to New York yet."

I hoped that there would now be a message from Daniel. Nothing. Daniel was obviously a lot less impressed by my shenanigans. Probably even majorly turned off despite his hard-on, which would have been a normal physical male reaction in any red-blooded man who wasn't gay. I mulled over Samuel's words. "Rambling Rose" . . . who, or what, was *Rambling Rose*? I had humiliated myself with Daniel. He was a *theater* director, with principles and standards.

Fiddling with my phone, I saw that Daniel

hadn't called my voicemail, but he *had* left a text. It read:

You're worth more than that, Janie. Don't sell your soul.

I felt I'd been stabbed. Only Daniel knew how to wound me so profoundly. But he was right. The direction this movie was taking was the opposite of everything I stood for. I didn't spend four years at Juilliard, probably the best damn drama school in the country, to simply rip off my clothes and act like a prostitute.

I called Pearl back. She didn't answer so I left a message.

"I'm so grateful for the chance," I said, "and I appreciate your interest, but what I did at our meeting was completely out of character for me, and it's a direction I don't want to pursue. I don't know what came over me, and I'm sorry I let myself get out of control. Please thank Mr. Myers but let him know that I do not want the role in his movie, as I do not believe I'm the right actor for the part. Thanks again, and it was great meeting you." I paused and added (so I didn't burn all my bridges), "I would love to work with you in the future if you have anything that suits me better. Thank you so much. Goodbye."

Star stared at me with an open mouth. "What the fuck was that all about?" She took a sip of her coffee and picked at a muffin. "Don't you think you should have chatted with me about this first? I mean, Samuel Myers may be a jerk but he is very powerful. Janie, you have sabotaged a great opportunity."

"An opportunity to behave like a slut? To flash my wares on screen in front of millions? That's just not me, Star. I trained and *trained* at drama school. Two toads terribly tired tried to trot to Tewkesbury."

She laughed. "*What?*"

"Grab the groundhog from the glazed grass. Around the rugged rocks the ragged rascal ran."

Star tried to say that sentence and failed miserably. We burst out laughing.

"Red lorry, yellow lorry, red lorry, yellow lorry, red lolly, yellow lolly," she blurted out, then laughed again.

Then I said earnestly, "Look, I didn't learn to enunciate my consonants, breathe from the diaphragm and learn reams of Shakespeare so I could then whip off all my clothes. It's not my ambition to be famous for the sake of being famous. I'm a serious actor."

"Whatever," Star said with a hurt look on her face.

I realize I'd insulted her. Not only was Star not a "trained" actor, but she had taken her clothes off once or twice in movies. But in her case it worked. Me? It would be my debut and something I'd never be able to shake off for the rest of my career.

"Let's go, or we'll be late," she said, getting up. "I have to collect my kids from their friend's house. First we need to swing by my place though."

Uh-oh, I'd unwittingly snubbed her. "I love your work, by the way," I said, to try and smooth things over. "Really, you made me cry ugly tears in *Skye's The Limit*."

WHEN I SET MY GAZE on Star's home, my nose prickled and my eyes welled up at its beauty. It was like something you'd see in an architectural magazine. She lived in Malibu, right on Pacific Coast Highway, her backyard a wild garden, and the beach her playground. There were olive and orange trees, and tropical grasses that sprung from the sand, climbing jasmine, sweet and aromatic, and a hammock above a wooden deck where you could laze and read books. There was even a pool, the water not bright turquoise but a gunmetal blue. The back of the house was a set of vast, sliding glass doors, leading from the enormous, state-of-the-art kitchen, and living room; the view spectacular. I breathed in the salty breeze. This place was heaven.

"You like our pad?" Star asked with a wink. "Not bad, huh? For a girl who grew up in a trailer park."

"You grew up in a trailer park? I never knew that."

"Before I became famous. Before we were financially solvent. You could have a place like this, you know, if you choose to branch out into movies."

"You mean, if I take my clothes off?"

"Hey, I've done some work I'm not thrilled with, but it paid the rent. It put food on the table. You can either go and read *Miss Julie* somewhere and study your craft 'til you're blue in the face, or you can get on board and make some real money."

I was surprised. I had believed that Star was an actress who held onto her ideals. Now, it seemed, as if she was advocating film, not as a craft, but as a vehicle for making money. But then, she'd been very poor, judging from her background. Poor is something you never forget. My damp apartment that had patches of mold growing on the ceiling came to mind. It was a "steal" by New York standards, even with the mold. I thought of my younger brother, Will, who—intellectually impaired and with mild autism—needed all the aid he could get. I helped him out financially whenever I could. And here was Star offering to give me a leg up, introduce me to her power agent, and make calls to Steven freaking Spielberg! And I was acting like a purist, a green ingénue, fresh out of drama school. I couldn't ride on my Tony nomination forever, yet at the same time, I didn't want to let go of my morals, my ideals, about who I was as an actor. At least, the type of actor I had always wanted to be. The sort who, as Daniel said, didn't sell her soul. I was one, screwed-up, hypocritical mess. Kissing Daniel that way, and at the same time saying I didn't want to play parts like that.

Who was I kidding? I needed to sort out my head.
And fast.

I smiled wanly at Star and came up with,
"Well, a girl can dream, right?"

Star took me by the wrist and looked me in the
eye. "Yes, Janie, a girl can dream, but a girl also
needs to *eat*. A girl needs to be practical. If you
don't want this particular part, fine. We can work
on getting more auditions, more meetings. I know
people, and I like you. I see your talent, I see
something rare in you. And I can help you. But
unless you are *with* me on this, I'd be wasting my
time."

"You want me to meet with your agent?"

"She's very influential. She has a lot of fingers
in a lot of pies. Your agent is good for theater, yes,
but not much more. Maybe they could work out a
deal so you don't need to actually fire yours. Look,
this world is tough, dog eat dog. You're young and
beautiful, but that won't last forever. You have to
strike while the iron's hot. Right now, you *are*
pretty hot because your performance is still fresh
in people's memories, but they suffer from amne-
sia in this town . . . before long you'll just be
another actress vaguely ringing a bell in their

subconscious somewhere. I know I sound like a bitch, but what I'm saying is true, believe me."

"I do believe you."

"You have a cute, sexy little body. So what if your breasts flash on screen for a few seconds! That's the European way. It didn't bother Keira Knightley or Kate Winslet. The American way is to have a boob job, then hypocritically encase those sexy boobs in a bra and boast about how you 'don't do nudity.' How fucked up is that? In Europe, kids frolic naked on beaches, women go topless. Nudity there is no big deal. If it's done in a classy way, what's the harm? That's my point of view, anyway. But if you really feel strongly about it you can get a body double. Julia did that for *Pretty Woman*. You can stipulate that in your contract. Work is work, stop being so precious about it. Do you want a house like mine, or not? Or do you want to wait tables in New York for the rest of your life?"

Wow, Star was like a mind reader.

"The last time I waited tables I got fired," I admitted.

"Well there you have it. Mull over what I've said. Think about it hard because the here and now is your chance. Not tomorrow, not the next day, not some hazy day in the future. Your decisions today will affect the rest of your life. Think, Janie, about what you actually want."

5

THAT NIGHT I TOSSED and turned like a wild animal in a cage. I could hear the waves slapping against the sand and seagulls crying out like cats in the night. After Star's pep talk all I could do was ask myself, over and over, what *is* it you want, Janie? And my pathetic answer came back to me: *Daniel Glass*. I wanted him more than anything else. More than a career. More than life itself. Seeing him again had undone me. I was a pathetic wreck. I hadn't been raised that way, to put so much importance in a man. My mother had drummed it into me that I needed to be independent, earn my own living, to never rely on the male species. For anything. She knew. My dad was the unreliable type and she'd spent the best part of their marriage holding the reins. My younger brother, too, needed guidance, protection. "Women are the stronger vessel," Mom always told me. "Hold onto your independence. Be a brick house, not a house of straw."

Yet here I was, back to square one, as if the last year without seeing Daniel had never passed at all. I was still the twenty-one-year-old, impressionable actress in my heart, eager to please. Desperate to earn his approval.

My mind wandered back to dinner, earlier that evening. Star and Jake were so in love. I craved a relationship like that. They were alive, sparring with each other over who was the better actor, Al or Bobby—*The Godfather* or *Taxi Driver*. But they were laughing and joking, her daughter Hero asking silly questions that made us all laugh.

"By the way," I had asked, "who's *Rambling Rose*?"

"Laura Dern was *Rambling Rose*. Great movie," Jake said. "She got nominated for an Oscar."

"Why rambling?"

"She was innocently promiscuous; mistook sex for love."

"She had rambling ways," added Star.

"Ah," I said.

"Why do you ask?"

"Because Sam Myers decided I was like her," I told them.

Rambling Rose . . . I lay in bed thinking again about Daniel's erection the moment I straddled him. *Surely* he felt something for me—his hard-on proved it, didn't it? He couldn't forever mourn his dead wife.

I wanted that role in the film after all. What had I been *thinking* to tell them no? Neither Pearl nor Samuel Myers had telephoned me back. I'd blown it. What an idiot! Lying here, I decided I would give my right arm to work with Daniel again. See his face every day on set . . . discuss my character's motivation, listen to and follow his direction. I could feel the familiar heat between my legs. I'd pleasured myself so many times in the past I couldn't count, fantasizing about Daniel fucking me. I hadn't even dated other guys. Well, I'd tried, but never got past a kiss. Nobody turned me on. Everybody was anemic and insipid compared to Daniel. No, it was sad and pathetic for me to get myself off yet again tonight, always obsessing about Daniel Glass. I refused to allow myself torture my poor humiliated body anymore with someone I couldn't have.

I got up out of bed and walked toward the big glass doors of my bedroom. There was enough moonlight to see a little without stumbling in the dark. Stars were scattered like tiny jewels in the sky, and I fancied I could make out the Big Dipper—a saucepan in the midst of the deepest blue. I picked up my iPhone and, taking it outside with me, found the astrology app that tells you what the constellations are. I lay down on the sofa and stared up at the sky in a trance.

A while later, fiddling with my phone and changing the angle, I suddenly realized there was a message. From Daniel.

Phone me. NOW.

Without pausing for breath I called, my heart racing. To my astonishment he picked up. What was he doing awake? I had his beautiful features in my mind's eye. His intense blue eyes, his straight nose, with that very slight bump, and his full, sexy lips that I had imagined a million times licking me all over, electrifying my body into orgasmic bliss.

"Janie," he said, in a low seductive voice.

"Daniel, I'm amazed you're still up."

"I can't sleep." He paused. There was a beat of silence and he said, "I've been thinking about your kiss. You got me fucking hard, you know that, don't you? Of course you do. It was embarrassing."

An arrow of desire shot to my core, remembering his hard-on. I had always pictured what his cock was like, but feeling it at the meeting against my legs, and seeing its solid ridge wedged against his slacks, I noticed that he was big. Very big.

"You were between a rock and a hard place," I joked.

"Not funny, Janie. It was humiliating."

"I'm sorry," I whispered.

"We need to talk."

"We could meet tomorrow. Star's got a meeting so I'll be alone all afternoon, you could pick—"

"Now. We need to talk now."

"Well, I can't sleep so . . ." *Can't sleep because of you,* I wanted to add, but I bit my lip to stop myself.

"Stop biting your lip and twiddling your hair, it's—"

"A bad habit," I said, finishing off his sentence.

"I wasn't going to say that actually."

"How did you know I was twiddling my hair?"

"Because I know you."

No, you don't, you don't know everything. "What were you going to say then, if it wasn't to tick me off?"

"I'll tell you when I see you. Where are you?"

"At Star Davis's house on Pacific Coast Highway. I'm in her backyard, listening to the crashing waves, staring at the stars in the sky. The real stars, not movie stars.

"I'm on my way over."

"What if I refuse to give you the address?" I taunted.

"I know the architect who built her house and I went to see it once, and I'm staying with friends who happen to live near you, just up the beach a ways."

"That's convenient."

"Yes, it is. Very."

I could hear measured panting. "Why are you breathing heavily? What are you doing?"

"Jogging along the beach. I'm on my way.

Won't be long." The phone went dead.

What did he want to talk about? Never had a person instilled such fear and desire all at once in me. He would berate me, tell me that he didn't want to work with me ever again, that what I did was cheap and tacky. God, I hated being an actor sometimes. The DNA of insecurity—part of a thankless job. Insecurity manifested itself in a myriad of ways; prickly behavior, promiscuity, bitchiness, cockiness, and often alcohol or drug abuse. I knew that Star once had a drug problem. Twice, three times actually—she kept relapsing. No actor gets off lightly, even when they're famous.

I looked back up at the starry void and must have dozed off, because the next thing I knew, Daniel was leaning down stroking my hair. I opened my eyes. I knew it was him because I could smell his familiar, masculine scent. His clean musty aroma that made me weak every time he came near me.

"So beautiful," he whispered.

"What?" I wondered if he was referring to the starry sky but he was looking at me directly.

"You woke a sleeping bear," he said. "You

know that expression, Let Sleeping Dogs Lie? The Swedish talk about bears, not dogs. You should have let me sleep, Janie, but you woke me up."

"When I responded to your text message?"

He chuckled. "No, when you kissed me and gave me a raging hard-on. You woke up my senses." He took my hand and brought it to his crotch. "Feel how hard you've made me again."

I breathed into his face, "Oh God!"

"I'm going to have to fuck you, because you've asked for it. It's what you've wanted all along, isn't it? To get fucked by me?"

I could feel his enormous erection through his jeans. It was almost intimidating. Almost. "Yes," I whimpered. "I'd like to deny it but that'd be a lie."

He leaned in closer and planted a light kiss on my forehead. "Not the innocent little girl we all thought now, are we?"

"No," I murmured.

"You're a fiery little tiger beneath that school-girl body, aren't you? I bet you're wet just thinking about how hard I am and how much I want you. Are you wet?"

He pressed his face against mine and kissed me, driving his tongue into my mouth and licking it, biting my lip softly, all the while groaning. His groans sent currents of lust through my body, hardening my nipples.

"Oh God," —I breathed into his lips— "Daniel." I flung my arms around his neck.

His hand gripped my ankle and then tantalizingly traveled up my calf, igniting every cell, every nerve along my sensitive skin.

"So soft, Janie." He let his fingers crawl higher, easing up, up, between the apex of my thighs. I opened them a touch to let his hand in. "Jesus Christ, you're soaking, baby." He plunged two fingers inside me and I cried out. This was the most sensual thing that had ever happened to me. I pushed my hips at him so he'd get in further. "So fucking horny for me, aren't you?"

"Yes," I admitted.

He started to finger fuck me, my juices swirling in celebration as he pumped me, his other hand rubbing my clit. I'd come any second if he carried on like this.

"I so want to fuck you, Janie. Lie on top of you and drive myself into your hot pussy. So you can feel every hard, thick, pumping inch of me. Make you scream. Make you come."

"Oh please!" I flexed my hips up at him as I thrashed frantically against the hand that was rubbing my clit with such expertise. One, two . . . I was going to come any second . . .

"But I need to know one thing first." His hand slowed down and so did my pulse. *NO! Not now! Keep going, please.*

"What do you need to know?" I panted, "please don't stop what you're doing."

"Are you in love with me?" His fingers were still inside me.

"Yes," I groaned, aching for him to finish off what he started.

"Then I'm not going to fuck you after all."

"What?" I screamed out, pushing my hips at him and pressing my own hands on his so he'd make me come.

"I'm in love with my late wife," he said quietly but not taking his hand away. He was still rubbing me slowly there . . . gently. The tease was driving me crazy. "It's not fair to you; I'd break your heart. I only fuck women I don't care about, and I *care* for you, Janie. I can't have sex with you, I—"

"Please, *please*, just make me come."

"Just this once. But it's the first and last time."

He prized my thighs apart and got down on his knees, then buried his head between my legs. He growled with animal pleasure, his sound stifled by me when I locked my thighs around his head. His tongue licked up and down my clit—"Fuck, Janie you're so sweet,"—and deep inside my opening, giving me the biggest orgasm of my life. I could feel tears awash on my face as I cried out in ecstasy, in pain—my climax breaking me into thousands of pieces, like shards of glass.

He continued pressing his tongue inside and then licked me up and down again, flicking and lashing at my clit like a mini whip. Another wave surged through me. This was unbelievable!

"I'm coming again!" I moaned.

I opened my eyes as another orgasm pulsed through me. It was light. No stars in the sky. An orange sun was peeping above the horizon. I was lying on my back on the sofa outside, my phone had fallen on the ground. The morning dew soaked my skin and I was damp all over, not just from the dew, but also with my own sweat. My hands were pressed between my sticky legs.

Daniel was not there.

I picked up my phone, my fingers fumbling,

frantic to find the "phone me now" message he'd sent. It was not there either. I got up and made my way through the garden towards the beach, my gaze manically searching the seascape and the back of the garden.

Of *course* Daniel couldn't have just come up from the beach and found me sleeping. This belonged to movie stars; there was major security! Locked gates sectioning off the beach from Star and Jake's backyard. *Daniel was not here last night!*

Except in my imagination.

I'd been fucking dreaming again.

6

I NEEDED TO TAKE control of my life—control of *myself*. I'd *had* it with these obsessive dreams of Daniel. They were stopping me from living, from getting out there and dating other guys. One part of the dream I suspected to be true, which made my situation even more ridiculous; he *was* still in love with his wife. I knew it, my subconscious knew it. And I'd heard as much through the grapevine.

Star found me in the kitchen, nursing a coffee at ten a.m. I had gone back to bed and slept like a baby, and only just showered fifteen minutes ago. I remembered I needed to call my dad and little brother, touch base back home.

"Wow, you're up late."

"You too," I remarked. Star was still in her bathrobe.

"Was your bed okay? The mattress not too soft, not too hard?"

"It was soooo comfortable, I want to kidnap it and take it back to New York."

I told Star the events of last night, that I'd crashed out on the sofa in her backyard, dreaming of Daniel. I omitted the "wet" part of the dream, of course. There were limits. But I did tell her, finally, about my general Daniel obsession, which had been going on since I was twenty-one. Two years of unrequited . . . *should I call it 'love?'*

"You've got it bad, huh?"

"I thought I'd gotten over him. It makes me so *angry* that he has this power over me!"

"I so identify."

"You do?"

"Yeah, Jake made me crazy at one point. All I could think about was him. Meanwhile he was fucking other women and drinking like a sailor, and showing me in every way that he was the last man on earth I should have been with. But then things turned around."

"So what did you do while he was being a

jerk?"

"Went away. Abroad, traveled round the world, incognito. Worked in an elephant sanctuary."

"Cool. Sounds amazing. Sadly, I can't do that right now, much as I'd love to."

"You need to go on some dates, Janie. Daniel's very handsome and charismatic and everything—I met him once—but there are other fish in the sea. Right now all you'd be is sloppy seconds. It's too soon; he must still be mourning his wife." She shook her head. "What a tragedy that was."

Her words reminded me of the very thing I wanted to forget. The wish I'd made, willing Daniel and Natasha to split up.

"I never seem to meet anyone I find really attractive," I lamented, "you know, someone who makes my heart race."

"That's because you live in New York. All the good looking guys in New York are gay. Or married."

I laughed. Star always got straight to the point. "I know," I groaned, "it's true. Every time I see someone hot, the second they open their mouth, the illusion is gone."

She padded over to the kitchen table and re-filled my coffee. "Have you tried therapy? I know someone who could help you."

"I need a *hypnotist* not a therapist. Someone to make me forget him completely, wipe him, not only from my mind, but also from my deep subconscious. Did you ever read *Midsummer Night's Dream*?"

"Course. Long time ago though."

"It's like that. As if someone put love juice on my eyelids while I was sleeping and the first person I saw when I woke up was Daniel. Like I have a spell on me. After we finished rehearsing, even when I knew he was getting married, I'd walk past his door in hope I'd bump into him. How sick is that? Like I was a glutton for punishment. Knowing he wasn't into me, yet praying somehow he'd change his mind."

"He must have given you some kind of come-on at some point or you wouldn't have been so hooked on him."

"I don't know. Maybe. Maybe not. He can't help having piercing blue eyes that shoot straight through to your soul." *And other places.* "It's like the classic student/teacher syndrome. A schoolgirl crush. Just because they show you some attention, your mind fancies there's mutual attraction, when in reality they think of you as a child."

Star reached up for a mug from the kitchen cabinet. The place was sleek, all chrome and white marble floors. Futuristic. It was a lot of prime real estate for someone of her age. I was impressed. "You want some muesli? Toast? I'll squeeze some orange juice."

"Juice would be great, thanks. Nothing to eat though. Maybe later. Sorry to go on, Star, I know I must be boring you."

"We've all been there. That's why I'm so glad to be married now even though Jake drives me nuts sometimes."

"Where is he by the way? And where are the kids?"

"You noticed the silence too, huh? They're on set."

"All of them?"

Star cut some oranges in half and put one into an old-fashioned juice press, drawing down a lever and emptying the juice into a large glass. "Yeah, they're all working today and I *love* it. Peace at last. Talk about keeping it in the family. Hero wanted to act, and anything Hero wants Leo wants too. This is the second movie in the trilogy—Jake said no at first, but they offered him so much money he couldn't refuse." She handed me a full glass of juice.

"Love your citrus squeezer."

"We keep electric gadgets to a minimum. Someone is always getting up at five a.m. to be on set, so we all learn to sneak around as quiet as mice. Did you check your voicemail by the way? I turned the ring off the landline—didn't want to be disturbed."

"No, why?"

"Because Pearl called my cell. Twice. I haven't listened to the messages yet but I'm wondering if she's trying to get in touch."

"With me? I doubt it."

"Well answer her. Not only is she a very cool person, but she's a big player too. I'm going to get dressed—help yourself to anything you want."

"Thanks, I will."

Star left the room, and I took my juice and coffee to my bedroom. I sat cross-legged on the mattress and stared out at the view. The sun was pretty high and had transformed into a glare so bright I had to look away. The ocean was a dark blue, the horizon a haze of paler blues and gradating turquoises melting into the sky. There were a few surfers dotted about in wetsuits, like bobbing seals. I wondered if there were any sharks in these waters. Wish I'd never seen *Jaws*. Despite the rubbery neck of the obviously fake shark in the movie, I still feared the ocean.

I picked up my phone. Again, I scoured through my messages, just in case the "**Call me. Now**" text really did exist.

No, it didn't. Of course it didn't. When would I *learn?*

I listened to my voicemail: "Janie, it's Pearl. Well, hon, you really have stirred things up with Sam. Telling him 'no' has piqued his interest more than ever. He even scoured YouTube and found the video clip of you in *Where The Wind Blows*. He was about to call your agent, but I told him he should clear it with you first. He is offering you big money, Janie. He wants to cast you in the lead. I agree you'd be perfect. Call me, we need to talk." *No mention of Daniel. Hmm, wonder why?*

The next was from Mr. Grease-Ball Big Shot himself. "Janie," he said with a snort. *At least he got my name right this time.* "*My* Rambling Rose. I get it. I insulted you. I'm sorry. Please forgive an old producer and let's call a truce. The show must go on. And Janie, *you are the show*. Or you could be. I'm a tit and ass man myself, so, you know, I didn't quite get you at first. But I do now. Call me, honey. We need to do business."

I stood up on the bed and pranced up and down punching the air, then stopped—didn't want to break Star's bed. But the grin on my face stretched so wide my jaw was beginning to ache. *Yes*!! They wanted me for the part. Holy smoke, this wasn't another of my dreams, was it? I pinched myself to make sure, then I saw Star standing by the doorway, smiling.

"I take it you have good news, judging by that inane smirk on your face?"

"Pearl says they have an offer, I'd better call her back," I said, grabbing my phone.

She prized the cellphone out of my hand. "Not so fast. I know I told you to call her back but . . . right now, as things stand? Let them stew a day longer."

"A whole day? It'll seem rude!"

"Trust me, the cooler you are, the higher the

offer. If they're talking *money* now, which they weren't before, that means they're worried. You told them 'no.' Your silence will make them open up to negotiation."

Negotiation? "I've never played this game before, it makes me nervous."

"That's why I need you to meet my agent today. I'll call—we can see her for a drink this evening, or have lunch. You need guidance. From now on, you do not discuss money. You are the show and your agent is the business."

"That's what Sam Myers said. That I'm the show. What's your agent's name by the way?"

"Cindy Specktor."

"She sounds frightening."

Star laughed. "Spektor with a K. No C. She *is* pretty intimidating though. But not with her clients. With us she's a pussycat, but let's just say she's the kind of person you want on your side."

"This is all so new to me. So surreal."

"This industry *is* surreal, get used to it."

"What about Paula, my New York agent?"

"Call her. But wait till you've seen Cindy first."

"Cindy might not be interested in me."

Star laughed again. "Boy, you really don't understand Hollywood at all, do you?"

"Do I sound naïve?"

"Naïve is good. Naïve sells, don't worry about it."

"You sound so . . ."

"Jaded? Tough? I'm a product of a greedy moneymaking machine, honey, that is called the movie industry. I can read it like an open book. Get dressed, we need to get moving. Put something sexy on. Not too sexy, remember, you're a brand now."

"A *brand*?"

"All actors are a brand whether they're aware of it or not."

"And what the hell is *my* brand?"

"Classy, sexy ingénue with social proof."

"What? You're crazy, what on earth is social proof?" I laughed, and opened my suitcase, wondering what I should put on to meet the infamous Cindy Spektor.

"You have proven talent because of bragging rights to a Tony nomination. Social proof. You don't need to persuade anyone you can act, the proof is already out there. Be ready in fifteen minutes." Star sashayed out of the room, her sky-blue silk robe trailing behind her.

Her observations got me thinking. I had never thought of myself as some sort of "product" before, and it scared me. But also made me remember what she'd said about waiting tables. This was my one big break. I had to do things right or my luck could splinter. I felt disloyal meeting a new agent before I had even spoken to mine, but Star was right; Paula was great for theater but little else. She wouldn't be able to swim with the Hollywood sharks, even rubbery-necked *Jaws* (Samuel Myers—fake and full of bullshit but still terrifying).

With all this swirling in my mind, I suddenly remembered I'd promised to call my dad when I arrived in LA and had forgotten with all the excitement.

My brother picked up.

"Hi Will, what's up? How's it all going?" Will had started a little business tutoring housewives with mastering the Internet. From learning to do basic stuff for the old folk like sending emails, to learning Photoshop and WordPress for women setting up online businesses, Will was the go-to guy. Or would have been, had his love for video games not gotten in the way. One woman had been taught to play "Call of Duty" when she had asked to learn how to manage her website.

"Dad's not home," he replied distracted.

"So what's up, anyway?" I said.

"What's down?" He liked to make that joke.

"What's the weather like back home?"

"You know, mud season. Mud season. Mud season."

"Yeah, I'd forgotten about that.

"Gotta go, Janie. You take care now, you hear?"

"Bye, Will, tell Dad to call me."

I knew that this newfound business of Will's wasn't going to last long. Too much responsibility. He was twenty-one, but had the mind of a fourteen-year-old. His clients were mostly friends of my dad's. But because of his autism it was doubtful he'd ever be able to hold down a regular job, and I always worried about how he'd manage financially in the future and wanted to help in any way I could.

Just then my phone buzzed.

It was Daniel.

My heart pounding, I picked up.

"Janie," he said. My adrenaline went from

naught to a hundred.

"Hi, Daniel."

"We need to talk." *Was this for real??* That's what he said in my dream—*we need to talk.* Just showed how well I knew him.

"I have an agent meeting later. I mean I *think* I do," I told him.

"You're being seduced, aren't you? By *them.*"

I laughed awkwardly. I wanted to tell him about my dream, how *he* was the one who'd seduced me. A thousand times, no less. "Seduced?"

"Don't lose your integrity, Janie Juilliard."

"I'll be okay, I have a great mentor, someone who can show me the ropes."

"Star Davis?" He laughed. "She comes from a different planet than you. She was *born* into this world. She's tough; it can't hurt her the way it can you. You are an *actor*, not a movie star or wide-eyed starlet. You deserve Broadway, the West End, the National, The Royal Shakespeare Company. You are worth twenty Star Davises. And I won't be there to protect you."

The idea that Daniel Glass wanted to protect me made my heart swell. "Why not? What about the movie?"

"I've pulled out. Samuel Myers and I do not see eye to eye. Pearl Chevalier seems to be on board with my artistic choices, but Sam Myers is a fat fucking philistine and I don't trust him an inch. His gig is all about money and nothing else. What started out as an art movie is quickly turning into a high budget sex romance. He's even talking about BDSM themes, for Christ's sake. He wants to compete directly with the *Fifty Shades of Grey* movie, which won't work as it's in a league of its own anyway. And he's adamant that you be his progeny, his star. That stunt you played at the meeting—at my expense—worked."

It wasn't a stunt, it was real. "I . . . I . . ." I stammered, "I don't know what to say. This is a big chance for me, Daniel. And I'm so sorry if I embarrassed you."

"It's fine. Water under the bridge. Meet me for a coffee, or lunch. See if I can't persuade you otherwise."

"I'll find out what Star's plans are and I'll call you right back," I said. "Thanks for calling."

My head was spinning with all this information. I felt elated, excited, yet at the same time deflated. I'd finally come around to the idea of

Daniel directing me again. Seeing him every day. Being mentored by him. But now I'd be on my own—well, I had Star to guide me, but it was true what Daniel said; she was used to this, it didn't faze her. I was just a tiny fish in a giant unpredictable ocean, with ruthless predators keen to gobble me up and spit the remnants of me right back out. Select my tasty bits and discard the rest.

I eyed my wardrobe choices. I picked out a pair of jeans and a little white tank. Some Converse sneakers. I put on my simple outfit and looked in the mirror. My nipples showed slightly through the shirt. No bra. Didn't need one. That, I decided, would be my "brand." The accidental sex symbol who dresses like a boy. Minimal makeup, minimal effort. Doesn't give a damn.

I contemplated the new direction I was taking in my career. For the first time in my life I considered what it was to be famous and more importantly, the money that would come with it. Able to pay my bills, help out my brother. I tasted it like the metallic taste of blood—dangerous, bad for me. But I wanted it anyway. I needed it.

And I was going to go after it.

Hollywood, here I come.

7

STAR LENT ME HER custom-made, sky-blue Porsche, which had a very fancy, integral GPS system. I had no idea where I was going so I drove blindly, following Snoop Doggy Dog's instructions (yeah, really), until I ended up on Mulholland Drive in the Hollywood Hills, where Daniel was staying at a friend's house. The friend was away indefinitely and had lent Daniel his home for as long as he needed it. My dream had me so convinced it was real that I was surprised that he was not staying in Malibu near me, "just up the beach a ways."

As I approached a pair of enormous iron gates, I hesitated, but they magically opened so I knew I'd come to the right place. The house was a swanky, Mediterranean style villa, with steps leading up to it, circular balconies, and a sweeping driveway big enough to accommodate a good forty or so cars. There were neatly trimmed hedges, Versailles style, and views looking to the mountains in every direction.

Daniel was standing on the steps, waiting for me. He was dressed in black. He often dressed in black. It suited his intense disposition. I could make out his pectoral and chest muscles beneath his T-shirt, his strong, tanned forearms—tanned from being here in LA—I supposed. He stood there, legs apart, not smiling, but his penetrating gaze told me he was glad to see me.

I pulled the car up and got out, swiveling my legs around as if I were wearing a short skirt—then remembered I was just wearing skinny jeans.

"It's seems incongruous, doesn't it?"

I cocked my head. "What does?" It was that awkward moment; the kiss on both cheeks. When we were rehearsing none of us ever did the thespian air kiss with Daniel. He didn't like it. He used to say, 'We see each other every day, for Christ's sake, save the lovey dovey daahling kisses for opening night.'

But he stepped down, put his arm around my shoulder and said, "Welcome to La La Land where you and I don't belong."

"How do you know I don't belong here?"

"Because I know."

"This place is outrageous," I said, doing a three-sixty. "So flashy!"

"Did you bring your swimsuit? There's a heated saltwater pool with cascades, and God knows what."

I hadn't brought my swimsuit, I wasn't sure how I'd feel being undressed in front of him, so I purposefully left it behind. "I forgot," I said. "How long are you staying in LA, then?"

"Only a couple more days. As I said, I'm bailing on the movie so there's no point being here longer."

"You could catch a few rays. Hang out a while."

"I don't 'hang out,' Janie, you should know that by now."

I smiled. "Yeah, I should know that by now. A girl can dream."

He turned to me, took me by the hand, and stared me in the eye a full ten seconds (which felt like a millennium) and said, "What *do* you dream about, Janie Juilliard?"

I could feel myself turning beet-red, from my toes all the way up to my hair, which felt like it was standing on end with the charge of electricity between us. *You, and little else.* "This and that."

He pulled me by the hand, leading me into the enormous circular foyer that shone marble, and twinkled with crystal chandeliers, and vast floor to ceiling picture windows. He had never held my hand before—well, once, just to lead me upstage during rehearsal, to show me where to stand. His hand was warm and firm, and I tried not to grip it too hard. His other hand he slid around my waist. I could sense myself tingling all over. "Well, I dreamt about *you,* Janie, last night."

What?? I couldn't answer, my mouth parted in shock. "And?"

"I was fu . . . following you," he said, and he swallowed hard. He narrowed his cerulean-blue eyes, locking his gaze on mine as if he were reading my thoughts.

"On a beach?" I suggested. Heat spiraled through my body. *I am not imagining this! Daniel Glass is flirting with me! He was dreaming he had sex with me*! *Fu . . . following me*!

He smirked ever so slightly. "No, not on a beach."

"Where?" I asked, way too eagerly.

He dropped my hand and took a step back as if to distance himself. "I can't remember."

Liar! "Because I dreamt about *you* last night," I confessed in a quiet voice, "what do you think that means, that we're dreaming about each other simultaneously?"

He shrugged. "Absolutely nothing. We saw each other yesterday, hadn't for over a year, and . . . well, it's normal, isn't it, that we should slip into the other's subconscious now and again? Come outside—we should take advantage of this sunshine while we can. Come. You want a drink? A Coke or something?"

"Sure," I said, feeling a little hurt at what he'd said. *'Slip into the other's subconscious* **now and again**.*'* If only he knew the extent of thought-time he inhabited in my brain. In fact, he had a whole mansion in my brain, exquisitely furnished, endless grand rooms, even ballrooms, wandering corridors, leading to more rooms, with French doors leading onto sprawling gardens—the view endless.

We passed by the kitchen and Daniel got some Cokes out of the fridge. *Classic* Coke. I knew better than to get him on the subject of Pepsi, or even Diet Coke. Daniel was a purist.

He clinked in some ice and slices of lemon and set the drinks on a tray. Even the simplest thing like preparing a couple of sodas was done with precision. The Daniel Glass way.

"Here, Janie." He handed me my drink, looking me in the eye again, and I saw a flash of sadness. There was something different about him. He seemed vulnerable somehow. Worse than vulnerable, *broken*. Then again, his wife had died. Normal. Although Daniel Glass and vulnerable didn't seem to go hand in hand.

We walked out to the pool, a kidney-shaped, shimmering expanse of water with an island in the middle.

"Who *is* this friend of yours who owns this crazy place?" I sat on a sun lounger.

"A guy in fashion, you wouldn't have heard of him. But he's rich as Croesus. He comes here, literally, a few weeks a year. He lives in Tuscany, London, Rome, New York. He's Italian and has always been extremely generous to me. He's one of our angels."

"Angels?"

"He's backed me several times with my productions."

I'd forgotten that term "angels" to denote a person who gave money to the theater simply for the love of it, asking nothing in return except a philanthropic love for the arts.

I took a sip of my Coke. "Not a bad friend to have then."

"So you're hanging out with that movie star, Star Davis?"

"Yes, I'm staying with her and her family," I said, twisting my hair up into a makeshift bun to get it off my neck.

"If you're hot, take your jeans off, don't mind me. I'm going to have a quick swim. Maybe I can find a spare swimsuit for you in the changing room."

"I'm fine, really." The truth was I didn't want Daniel to see my pale legs. I suddenly felt self-conscious about what I'd done in that meeting yesterday. "Daniel, I apologize if I embarrassed you in front of Pearl Chevalier and Samuel Myers."

"Actually, it was quite amusing." His lips tilted

into an ironic smile.

"Really? You don't hate me?"

"I could never hate you, Janie Juilliard."

"I don't know what got over me, it wasn't planned—"

"When that fat fuck insulted you, I nearly got up and punched him. But what you did was better. Far better. The only problem is that now he's obsessed with taking you away from me."

Is Daniel Glass *possessive* of me? My stomach flipped. "Taking me *away* from you?"

"He'll make you a big star. And you'll be famous. And the rest of Hollywood will come crashing at your door. You won't be bothered with doing theater anymore."

"That's not true!"

"Your tits will be up there, larger than life, your ass, your mouth. This movie's going to make you a sex symbol—are you ready for that?"

Are *you* ready for it? I wanted to say, judging by his mini outburst. Was he *jealous*? "Daniel, the whole thing might be a huge flop. I know you think I'm selling my soul, but I won't be. It might lead to other roles."

"Of course it'll lead to other roles. More of the

same. It pains me to see such talent thrown out the window."

"It's a chance for me, which I may never get again. Anyway, I still haven't told them yes."

He exhaled a breath of relief. "How much are they offering?"

"I don't know yet. I haven't called Pearl Chevalier back."

"Strategizing, are we?"

"Star told me to let them stew a while, that they'd offer more."

"And that they will, my girl, and that they will."

"Daniel, if this was such a crap project, why were you involved in the first place?"

"Because they gave me the impression that I'd have artistic control. That's how I got you through the door in the first place. I had plans to make a beautiful, artistic, and extremely sexy love story. Sometimes less is more. Suggestion is the key, not exploitation. But the next thing I knew, Sam Myers was bulldozing my ideas and vision. I'd forgotten how the Hollywood machine works. If things are controversial now, it'll only get worse. I bowed out before things got ugly. The only problem is I didn't expect them to snap you up like a bunch of greedy magpies. It was that damn kiss that did it!"

This was my moment. I had nothing to lose. I had to ask him directly. "Daniel, did you enjoy that kiss?"

He bit his lower lip. Picking up on my bad habits?

"What do *you* think?" he said.

"I saw the kind of physical reaction you got, so yes, I think you did secretly enjoy it."

"I fucking loved it, Janie," he said, staring me hard in the eye. "But I'm not going to act on it."

"Why not?"

"Because . . . look . . . for several reasons."

"Your wife?"

"Yes."

"And?"

"I'm feeling very angry right now. I'm in no state to have a relationship, least of all with you."

I felt the dagger going in. It was bad enough in my dreams, but this? This was *real*. I knew about feeling angry; when my mom died that was my prime emotion. It shouldn't have been, but it was. But Daniel talking to me as if I were the last person alive whom he'd consider having a relationship with, hurt like hell.

I got up. "I think I'd better leave," I said, looking at the ground. "I've humiliated myself enough already."

"*Humiliated* yourself? Janie, you've got the wrong end of the stick!"

"I know your wife was a fucking Amazonian goddess with beautiful big breasts and luscious blond hair and legs that went on forever and—"

Daniel sprang from his sun lounger and grabbed me close to him, squeezing me against his hard frame, his arm encircling my waist. With his other hand he held me firmly by the back of my head, his fingers laced through my hair. I was trapped. His lips centimeters from mine.

"Janie, you've got it all wrong; you have no idea what you mean to me, do you? No fucking idea at all."

And that's when it happened. *That* kiss.

I leaned into him, the echo of his words sending me into a sort of swoon. Our lips touched. It started as a soft tease, his tongue caressing my bottom lip, but then I opened my mouth, my tongue tentatively reaching out to his. He groaned, pressing his hardness against me as he licked into my mouth. He gripped my waist tighter as if afraid I'd slip away. His licks got faster, so sensual, so sexual that I could feel a gush of wetness gather hot between my legs. Then he took my lip between his teeth, nipping it, then sucking it into a deep kiss 'til our tongues were tangled together in a frenzy. We became wild, fucking each other with our mouths. Tongues, lips, teeth, his hand still gripping the back of my head—his prisoner. Yet I, so, *so* willing.

My body lost all strength of its own as I succumbed to Daniel completely. I could feel his erection, relentless, as his hand slid down from my waist and cupped my ass.

"Oh God," I moaned.

Our lips feasted on one another, hot and wet. His groans were like an elixir, urging me to give into him more by the second, which I did. Daniel Glass was irresistible. His blue eyes seared into me. Sexually fierce. Commanding. Demanding.

Fire.

Ice.

Death.

Life.

He terrified me with his intensity. I knew this

could be the end of me, but I couldn't let go. His kisses were a force of nature, his groans guttural, hungry, ferocious. As if he owned me.

Well, he did. He did own me.

I melted into him as if we were one being, saturated by his aura, the scent of him seeping into my every pore, weakening me, strengthening me. The flavor of his taste made me know in that instant that nobody could ever fill my senses with so much ecstasy as Daniel Glass. I let him suck on me, sucking out my shallow breaths as if they were my last. I could have died in that kiss and I wouldn't have even been aware. He was the vampire, and I his food. I didn't care.

That's how hopelessly lost I was with this man.

I heard my cell go and had every intention to ignore it. But it jolted Daniel out of the moment like an intruding alarm bell. He drew his head back. I could still feel the solid ridge of his cock pressed up against me, and I knew what I was going to do next: lie back on that sun lounger and let him take all of me. Every single inch of my desperate, pleading body. I could feel another surge of wetness pooling between my thighs. I'd never felt so ready.

"Janie," he said. His eyes were smiling although his mouth didn't tell the same tale. "I need to cool off."

What? He took his arm away from my waist, released my head, and before I could say a word, ripped off his T-shirt, kicked off his jeans, and dove into the pool.

I grabbed my cell. Furious with it for interrupting me. It was Star.

"Hey," I said in a curt clip.

"Janie, is he coming on to you by any chance?"

"Maybe." I watched Daniel as his streamline body cut through the water in a fast crawl.

"You need to leave, babe."

"I don't think I'm going anywhere right now."

"Okay, let me get straight to the point. You know I said you'd be sloppy seconds?"

"Yes, but—"

"You'd be sloppy tenths," she interrupted.

"*What* are you talking about?"

"Daniel Glass is on a pussy rampage right now. Word has it—even in the last couple of days? He's fucked like, three women."

"But that's not his style," I hissed into the line, "and he's still mourning his wife!"

"Open up your big brown Bambi eyes and listen to me. I have this from a seriously sound source. Daniel is *majorly* fucking around right now. His wife is dead, he's hurting, and he's on a roll. I do *not* want you to be another notch on his bedpost."

Jealousy seared me like a scalding iron. "Who? Who's he fucked?"

"Tall blond actresses and models. All Natasha Jürgen lookalikes. He gets to cherry pick. In Hollywood, being a director is akin to being a Greek god. Or a king. Even for the pockmarked ugly ones. But for someone as good looking as *Daniel Glass*, women—particularly wannabe starlets—wait in line. Around the block. Apparently he has a huge dick too, and they're screaming for seconds, but he's loving and leaving them and acting like a prize jerk. Janie, keep *away* from him until he gets this fuckathon out of his system."

My eyes strayed back to Daniel, who had just gotten out of the pool. His body was cut like the fine piece of Glass it was. His legs, strong and muscular, his ass tight and oh, just so *right*. It made me sick to think he was screwing around. Yet not with *me!* Daniel, a promiscuous player? It just didn't suit his personality. But Star was right. I couldn't risk it. Just one chastising look from him could send me into a post-mortem for days. Even weeks. If I had sex with him and then he ignored me afterward, it would destroy me. I had to stay strong, no matter how tempting he was.

I eyed him up as he grabbed a towel, water dripping off him like shining crystals. Fuck, he was handsome. Beautiful. Men just weren't made like him anymore. No, they looked too "done" these days, too pampered, like they'd made a ton of effort looking into a mirror and preening themselves—shoving products in their hair. Even shaving their chests and balls. So unmanly! So self-obsessed. Not Daniel—he was naturally good looking without having to try—pure one hundred percent tough, alpha male, every last inch of him, especially where it counted most. I wanted to explore him, immerse myself in him, but I knew how dangerous he was. At least, for me.

He sauntered toward me, smiling, his straight white teeth the only part of him that looked wholly American. He'd once told me he was a mixture of Italian, Cherokee, Irish, Scottish, Polish, and English. He was mysterious, ruthless, kind, unrelenting, unusual, and most importantly, his mind worked like nobody I had ever known. He was a one-off, an anomaly, and boy, was I hooked. It wasn't just his body, his beautiful face, and his intelligence that had me entranced—it was his soul. Even the darkest part of his soul.

"Star, I've got to go," I whispered into the phone.

"I mean it, Janie. If anybody knows what directors are like, it's me. Girls wet their panties over men like Daniel, and ninety-nine percent of single men cannot resist hungry, sexy big-titted starlets. Trust me. Keep. Away."

"I'll be home soon," I said, my eyes still roving over Daniel's lithe body.

"No, not home, meet me in a hour—you, Cindy, and I are doing lunch. I'll text you the address of the restaurant. Bye, hon."

I pressed END.

"Daniel, I'm off," I told him in an easy voice, or at least I tried to make it seem that way. Actually, I probably sounded pretty shaky.

He didn't reply, just looked at me, his expression giving nothing away. He was in his swim trunks, dripping wet. I noticed his beautiful feet—

even his toes were a fucking work of art.

"I'm meeting Star's agent," I explained.

"Cindy Spektor?"

"Yes, how do you know?"

"Because she wants to represent me. I met with her yesterday, as a matter of fact."

"Oh, cool. What's she like?"

"Tall, blond, imposing, and *very* determined to get her way." His mouth tilted into what I interpreted as a smirk.

I could feel my lips tighten, my chin strike a haughty pose. One of his fucks, for sure! I already hated Cindy Spektor and I hadn't even set eyes on her. I couldn't contain the hostility in my tone. "And? Are you going to sign with her?"

"Would it bother you if I did?" Obviously I wore my heart on my sleeve—he knew me too well, or at least, he could gauge my emotions.

"Of course it wouldn't bother me," I lied. "Make whatever choices you see fit." Again, my words as bitter as a triple espresso.

"Well, I'm in no rush." He took a step forward, a trace of a smile edging his lips. I needed to get away from him before he had me on my back, legs akimbo, begging for round two.

"So what are your plans then, if you're no longer doing the film?" I fired out, turning to go.

"I'm going back to New York."

I made my way to the hallway as he followed me. Then I turned to face him and said, "By the way, does the movie even have a working title? And if you're not directing it, who is?"

"You'll have to ask them. I'm out, I have no idea who they'll approach next. As far as a working title is concerned they were brainstorming yesterday, after you left, and came up with *The Dark Edge of Love*. Janie, is something wrong? You seem agitated. Why are you rushing off so fast?"

"I'm fine, just running late. Nice to see you, Daniel, see you around."

He grabbed me by the wrist. "See you *around*? What *is* this? Who was that on the phone? You seem . . . I don't know . . . pissed off with me in some way, all of a sudden."

I held his gaze. "When you have this whole *thing* out of your system, give me a call."

"This . . . '*thing*?' You're referring to my wife's *death*?"

Boy, I sounded crass and unfeeling. "I mean all the *side* effects her death is causing," I quickly amended. *The fact you can't keep it in your pants.*

"Janie, the situation is very different from how you imagine, trust me." He drew me close to him again, his cool, wet hand sliding along my arm.

The "situation." The fuckathon, you mean, as Star so aptly described it. "I really have to go, Daniel." I pulled my arm away.

"I'm sorry if I came on too strong, I just thought after yesterday's kiss—"

That I was an easy target. Your next fuck nicely lined up. "Yesterday's kiss," I cut in, "was a mistake." The words flew out of my mouth before I could stop them.

"I'm sorry," he said, and cast his eyes down. I knew that game—the game men so often play when they want to get into your panties; the *I'm just a sweet puppy dog and you've hurt my feelings* manipulation tactic. I wasn't buying it. This man was in *no way* ready for a relationship—he'd even said so himself! Yet I'd been so close to falling into my own trap. Luckily, Star had shoved some strong coffee under my nose and I had woken up with a jolt. Now *compos mentis,* I sure as hell wasn't going to be his one-night stand—worse, one-*afternoon* stand—one of his many hook-ups, his sloppy tenths or elevenths.

"I'll let you know how the negotiations go," I said coolly. "And what I think of Cindy Spektor." I spat out the word Spektor without meaning to.

"Give me a hug before you race off," Daniel implored, following me through the front door, a look of incomprehension on his flummoxed and furrowed brow.

I turned around, blinking so he couldn't see the tears well up in my eyes, as I let him put his arms around me. He smelled so good. I discreetly breathed him in.

"You're special, Janie Juilliard. Don't let them ever tell you otherwise." Hugging me close, he whispered in my ear, "Please stay longer. Stay with me. Please don't go."

I had to muster all my strength to pull away. "Sorry, I just can't." And I dashed down the steps of this grand Italianate mansion and jumped into Star's convertible, fired it up and sped off before he could persuade me otherwise.

Once safely out of the grand gates, and zipping around the precariously curvy mountain road of Mulholland Drive, I pulled over and got out my cellphone. I killed the engine. I still had plenty of time before lunch and my motor-mind couldn't get off the subject of Natasha Jürgen. Punishing myself, I Googled her. There were pages and pages of images. Red carpet; stunning in various designer gowns. Smiling, resplendent, glimmering. Ophelia in *Hamlet*, Nina in *The Seagull*. Modeling photos. In every picture she looked so beautiful. Wavy blond hair cascading over her shoulders. Her full, natural bust evocative yet classy. She was that rare combination of sex siren and beauty all in one. Daniel must have been besotted with her; she'd be a tough act to follow for any woman.

I pressed "Web."

Wikipedia sprang onto the first page. I clicked on it:

Natasha Katrine Jürgen (1979 – 2014) was a Tony Award-winning stage and screen actress and a former fashion model. In 2000 she came to prominence and critical acclaim in the theatrical production of Hamlet when she played Ophelia, being one of the youngest recipients ever to win the prestigious Theater World Award for her performance. Other awards received were The Critics' Theater Circle Award for the leading role in Antigone, and a Drama Desk Award for her role of Cordelia in King Lear.

Early life.

Jürgen was born in San Diego, California, the daughter of Helen Jürgen, a homemaker, and Steven Jürgen, a lawyer and business owner. Her maternal grandparents were from Germany and Sweden. She was raised in Springfield, Connecticut, with her older sister, Kristin, now a neurologist.

Modeling career

At the age of 15, Jürgen entered the Casablanca Modeling Agency's Look of the Year contest and was chosen first runner-up. The following year, she went to Milan, Italy, to pursue her modeling ambitions. At 16, she was featured on her first magazine cover, the Italian edition of Vogue. Several more magazine covers followed and Jürgen went on to do television commercials for products such as L'Oréal, and editorial campaigns for Roberto Cavalli, and Burberry London. Her modeling career established, Jürgen moved on to a career in film, her first serious role, playing the lead Jacqueline in *In Your Dreams,* where she was spotted by theater director Gavin Black, who cast her as Ophelia in Hamlet, which was the beginning of a long illustrious theatrical career.

My eyes scanned down all the endless theater and film credits until I landed on her personal life.

Personal life
Jürgen was married to theater director Daniel Glass from 2012 to 2014. They did not have any children although it was rumored that she was pregnant at the time of her death. She tragically died of an epidural hematoma after being hit by a bicycle while crossing the road in Central Park in 2014.

I didn't go over the details of the "Injury and Death" part that followed. I'd read the story a hundred times. But the *pregnancy*? *That* wasn't on Wiki the last time I looked! I felt faint. She was *pregnant*? Poor Daniel, not just losing his wife, but his baby too. Not only had I jinxed Natasha, but an innocent baby! No wonder his head was all over the place right now. And I had been responsible, with my *wish-they'd-split-up* thoughts.

But my sympathy and self-hatred soon morphed into jealousy at the thought of someone else bearing Daniel's child. I was sick. Mentally unhinged. Identifying with Glenn Close in *Fatal Attraction*, even. *Shut up already about Daniel Glass, Janie*! He was off limits! Yes, he'd said flattering things to me, but he had probably done the same with all the other women on his roll call. Men like him were used to getting anything and anyone they wanted.

I put down my phone, took in a deep breath, and sank, defeated, into my seat. Daniel had it all: brains, wealth, sophistication, beauty, talent, the works. I was just his little actress in his eyes. I *had* to get him out of my mind before I drove myself crazy!

I needed to get a grip, get on with my life and seize the opportunities given to me without sinking into marshmallow-brain-land when it came to Daniel.

I started the car and continued my drive. The sun was beating down and I welcomed every second of it. How many actors were given the chance I was being offered? One in a zillion! And there was no way I was going to let my obsession with Daniel spoil my chances.

8

I WANTED TO HATE CINDY, but I couldn't. She was friendly and had a fun sense of humor. Blond, busty (LA style busty—we all know what that means), she carried a cute Chihuahua named Ditzy, with a pink, diamante collar. Perfect, manicured nails (both the dog and her owner). A two thousand-dollar purse. The type of woman who was tough enough to have a one-night stand and not let it bother her. The sort who would initiate sex on the first date, have some fun and then move onto the next guy, maybe even negotiating a deal while she was at it, without blinking an eye. She was a warrior, a hustler, a businesswoman who put emotions on the back burner. At least, that's the impression she gave. I so wanted to ask her directly about Daniel, but when I brought him up, she just said, "He is *quite something* that Daniel Glass and I want him on my *books!* We'll see."

"He mentioned you hooked up yesterday," I ventured, the "hooked up" purposefully ambiguous.

She grinned and said, "We sure did, but you know, he doesn't feel like *committing* right now. I'll keep in touch with him though—you can lead a horse to water but. . . " –she fixed her gaze on me and added—"which brings me to *you*, sweetheart, we need to talk about *your* future!"

I decided to drop the Daniel subject—if she'd fucked him that was her business, not mine. I smiled at her, forgiving her in my mind for trespassing on what I ridiculously, psychopathically believed to be my property.

Star broke in, "Cindy can help you seal a lucrative deal. They'll be banking on you being overcome with excitement at being offered a movie. It happens all the time when someone comes from a theater background. Often the actor is so desperate for the part, they offer to do it for scale. The money sounds like crazy money compared to what they've been earning. You need to stay cool, Janie."

"I can negotiate your deal," Cindy suggested. "Studio cost-cutting has meant that mid-level stars are being nickel-and-dimed in ways that would have been unheard of in the past, and we don't want that to happen to you, Janie. Right now, they may be tempting you with big bucks, but when it comes to the small print they may try and skimp and save. We need to make sure you get those extra perks, residuals, and expenses, and that you aren't minimalized in any way."

"Minimalized?"

"Billing. You want top billing."

"What about nudity? I don't feel comfortable taking off my clothes."

"Fine, I have a great entertainment lawyer who can go through your no nudity clause with a fine toothcomb."

I sighed with relief. I trusted Daniel to make the film tasteful concerning nudity, but who knew in what direction it would go now?

"When we spoke yesterday," I said, "at the meeting with Daniel, we were discussing using improvisation as a vehicle for the movie, but now

I don't even know who the director *is*. Will there be a script?"

"All this I can discuss with the producers. Basically, I need to know if you are seriously interested in this project before I start playing hardball."

I reminded myself that I had a massive student loan to pay off. And I thought of Will. Dad was pretty useless—ever the penniless guitarist mentality, despite the fact his bespoke furniture workshop was doing okay. Will was only twenty-one but soon he'd be a man. He needed guidance. Financial stability. He hadn't gone to college because of his autism. Since mom died, I had taken her place.

"Yes," I told Cindy. "I definitely want the job."

OVER THE NEXT FEW DAYS, Cindy negotiated with Sam Myers, Pearl Chevalier, and the money people. She had come to an arrangement with Paula, my New York agent, that Paula would continue to represent me for all theater worldwide, and any television in New York, and that Cindy would handle everything else. I was a little cog in a massive wheel, with a team behind me, including an attorney. It was daunting but exciting too. I felt so professional.

They did do a screen test in the end, and Pearl told me that it had come out even better than they hoped. They wanted to see what actor would pair well with me, although they still hadn't chosen anyone. The script was now underway—the whole artsy, improvisation idea that Daniel had was abandoned. And Daniel went back to New York, glad, it seemed, to have escaped the mayhem and intrigue of *The Dark Edge of Love*.

As much as I was glad to move forward, the idea of Daniel going back to New York, and not doing the movie, haunted me. He was the only director I truly trusted. He always made the right choices, he could always help with the motivation of a character. Quite simply, he was the best.

The casting directors were on the hunt for the perfect sex-god to play opposite me. They had been seesawing between someone very famous and a newbie. Pearl liked the idea of two new faces, of creating new stars. Samuel Myers wanted box office all the way but was also trying to squeeze every dime out of the budget and was reluctant to come up with a multi-million dollar fee. Because he had a bee in his bonnet about hiring only me (as he felt he had "discovered" me), Cindy was able to get me a million dollars—unheard of for an actress starting out in movies. The buzz was out and people's expectations were already high. I went around with knots in my stomach—fear mixed with excitement. I ran along Malibu Beach screaming till my lungs burst about the million dollars. Daniel not being able to share this joy dampened it just a bit, but hey? How many actors get paid ONE MILLION DOLLARS for a role?

Star and her family went off for a weeklong vacation, leaving me at their house alone. New scripts were arriving by messenger every day, tweaked each time, till finally, they settled on what they said would be the final copy.

I lay back in a bubble bath, reading it, trying to work out the tone of the story.

```
FADE IN:

INT. BEDROOM - NIGHT

A naked young woman is bent over
the bed, her hands cuffed togeth-
er, a blindfold on her face. She
```

is in her early twenties, with long red hair. A man – tall, handsome and rugged, and holding a whip, is standing over her, whispering in her ear.

EXT. STREET – DAY

A woman with long brown hair is walking down Fifth Avenue. The street is crowded. The shop windows are decorated for Christmas. The same man we saw before, Jonathon, is running after her shouting the name of Sylvie. He overtakes her and realizes that she isn't who he thought she was.

INT. BEDROOM – DAWN.

Jonathon is putting on his slacks. A blonde is sleeping in a four-poster bed. He grabs his shoes and socks off the floor and quietly sneaks out of the room.

BLONDE
(Mumbles into pillow) Hey, where are you going?

JONATHON
I warned you I never stay over.

I took a swig of wine, eased back into my frothy bubbles, and continued reading. So far, this Jonathon character was a jerk womanizer—that much I'd gathered. He was screwing around big time. My character, Sylvie, hadn't appeared yet, but I guessed that at a million dollars my role had to be important. Obviously there were BDSM themes . . . would I end up getting bruised?

Perhaps Jonathon had dead wife issues like Daniel, and like Daniel, was on a fuckathon to try and numb his brain from depression. Sex was good for that—at least that's what I'd heard; sex addicts didn't do it for the sex alone but because it validated them and took their minds off the real problem. Just the *thought* of Daniel fucking around made my insides clench.

Relationships are all about timing. In general, when men get married it's not just because they fall madly in love. No, it's because there's a chip in their brain that tells them they are ready to settle down. To commit. Tells them they are *ready* for love and it's okay to let go. Meet the right man at the wrong time and you're screwed. Some lucky woman would meet Daniel in five years, when he'd be ripe to start afresh, by which time I would have long since given up. At least I hoped so, for my own sanity.

My mind wandered back to the casting of Jonathon. What actor would they choose? I hoped to God he wouldn't have bad breath or something. We were going to have to kiss with tongues, feel each other up. The camera was only allowed to catch a flash of my side boob—or at least that's what would appear on the big screen—but I'd still be topless, save tiny nipple covers, and with just the skimpiest flesh-colored covering down below. I needed to get over myself and stop worrying. Nicole Kidman had appeared naked on stage in *The Blue Room,* in London, early in her career. Lots of actresses had taken off their clothes for the sake of art. But would this be art?

The thought, though, of Daniel in New York, and me here, being directed by a stranger, left me to wonder . . . what would have happened if things had worked out how they were meant to? Daniel was judging me for taking the role, but he didn't know what it was like to need money the way I did.

It's easy to have highfaluting morals when you're rich.

Still, as much as I reveled in my newfound success, I secretly wished he was along with me for the ride.

9

M Y FIRST DAY ON SET was terrifying. Film wasn't like theater. They put a bit of silver duct tape on the floor, which you had to reach every single take but without looking down. Casually walk to "hit your mark" as if it was the most natural thing in the world, making sure you stood not an inch away from it. Filming is mechanical; your body has to be at the perfect angle, your eye line hitting the perfect spot, not too far left, not to far right. The crew talked about "crossing the line" which meant that the cameras stayed on one side so you couldn't double back on an action, or move in the opposite direction, or when it came to the cutting room the scene would be all over the place. Everything took hours to set up.

Only two minutes screen time took all day to shoot. I was exhausted and I'd hardly done a thing.

I was so nervous that I hardly had time to study my co-star, who had not been there for the read-through the week before. His name was Cal, aka Jonathon. Like me, he wasn't a movie star, e.g. was an "unknown," although he'd done reams of TV series and commercials. He didn't appear nervous though, had an easy manner and an engaging smile. Thank God. The last thing I needed was some sort of diva.

Cal and I were sitting in my trailer, playing Backgammon. Star had given me a tip before filming began. She told me, "Keep your tablet and phone off set and only glance at messages once a day. You'll need to concentrate and make friends. Get to know every last person's name, the gaffers, the grips, and electricians, even the runner. Don't sit in your trailer alone. Socialize. These people will be your family for the duration of the shoot, and sometimes for life."

I shook the dice. Two sixes. I smirked.

"You're on a roll," Cal said with a wink. "Make the most of it, babe."

I moved my piece. There was something

charming about Cal, so I didn't mind him calling me "babe." He was tall and slim but with a worked-out body, and so good looking he looked like a model, but his manner was a touch goofy, like he didn't take himself too seriously. A kind of brotherly type—perhaps the kind of brother Will could have been if he weren't emotionally "not quite all there." I never used the word "mentally handicapped" about my brother—for some reason I couldn't, I just thought of him as less attuned than most people. But having a normal conversation with Will was not easy. His mind wandered.

"Lucky I'm getting double sixes," I said to Cal, "because I can hardly concentrate on this game. Shouldn't we be going over our lines together instead?"

"You heard what Simon said. Wants it to be fresh, not over rehearsed, spontaneous."

Simon was our director, the one who'd taken Daniel's place. So far, so good. He was friendly at least.

"I'm just so used to blocking the whole play, scene by scene," I said. "Not 'play,' I mean script, movie, whatever . . . this seems—"

"Surreal?" Cal suggested.

"Yeah, surreal is a good word. I mean, half of me is over the moon, but at the same time I didn't figure on all this hanging around, waiting to work, while they fiddle with lights and camera angles. I mean, I feel guilty for our poor stand-ins. They must be dying of boredom doing nothing under the lights all day."

"They're getting paid for it, don't feel bad. I was a stand-in, once, years ago—it was my first job in Hollywood. It's not a bad gig."

"Oh yeah? Who for?"

"Ashton Kutcher. Orlando Bloom another time."

I studied his liquid brown eyes, his even features and strong square jaw. "Yeah, I can totally see that."

"Anyway, they get paid pretty good money and it's better than a lot of jobs."

"If Daniel were here, I'm sure he'd be doing it differently."

"What's it like working with the great Daniel *Glass*?" Cal asked. "I heard he was a bit of a tyrant."

"He's strict," I admitted. "But more because he's a perfectionist than anything else. He has a vision. Your turn. I just took you."

I handed Cal the dice and our fingers touched, his lingering for a second too long. "God, you're beautiful," he said, staring into my eyes.

I laughed. "Do you say that to all your leading ladies?"

He laughed too, his wide, friendly smile making dimples in his cheeks. "Yes, I do. Breaks the ice."

"You think I'm frosty?"

"No, I didn't mean that. But you are a little nervous. Don't be, you're a great actress."

"How do you know?"

"I saw you in *Where The Wind Blows*. I was in the first row. Saturday matinee."

"Get outta here! Is that another of your pick-up lines?"

"Could be. What do you think?"

"I think you're full of shit, Ashton. I don't think you saw me perform at all!"

"Okay, you got me. But I did Google you, and I did check out that video clip of the play, all five minutes of it, so in effect, I saw you. And I thought you were great. Your move by the way."

"Are you nervous about our sex scenes?" I

asked him.

He templed his large hands against his lips and studied me. "If it were just you, me, and the director, fine, but that big hairy cameraman with that big-ass lens?"

"His name's George."

"Yeah, George . . . well, I'm not so sure that I want him doing a close up on my pecker, you know? I think that could really dampen the moment."

"Dampen the moment?"

We both burst out laughing.

"You ever go nude on stage before? Or kiss, or anything?" he asked.

"I once had to take my panties off. But I was wearing a skirt so nobody saw a thing, and I had another pair underneath so it was cheating really. The audience gasped though—they were fooled. You?"

"A lot of kisses, simulated sex once, but sex wasn't the whole theme of the movie like this is. It was a rom-com so it was a little less intimidating."

"*You?* Intimidated?" I exclaimed. "You don't give off that vibe at all."

"I'm an actor. Fooling people is my job." He

winked at me again.

"I know. When people ask me what I do for a living sometimes I tell them, 'I lie.' Their reaction always makes me laugh."

"So, apart from being a terrible liar, what else can you tell me about yourself, Janie?"

"Well, I graduated from Juilliard with honors and—"

"Not all the actor crap, but about *you*. Where were you raised?"

"In Vermont, born in England."

"You get to have a British passport?"

"I do. Dual citizenship. One of my dreams is to work in the West End or join the Royal Shakespeare Company, so it's an extra string to my bow."

"Which side is British?"

"My mom's."

"Does she have a British accent?"

"She did. She died a few years ago."

"So sorry."

"Yeah, it sucks." I looked away, desperate not to think about her, so changed the subject back to Cal. "How about you? Where are you from? I forgot to Google you."

"Isn't it the worst? That we can all go around stalking each other these days? No guessing, no romance left. No intrigue, no finding out about someone little by little. I admit I looked your work up, Janie, but I didn't do the full stalk." Was he being serious or kidding? His face was deadpan, then he added, "You dating?"

"No, you?"

"My girlfriend and I split up three months ago."

"Oh, sorry about that."

"Yeah, well, three's a crowd."

"Three?"

"She was cheating on me with my best friend."

"Oh my God! How awful, that must hurt like hell."

He nodded. "I forgave him, you know? He's a guy who can't keep it in his pants, so eventually I had to let go."

"*Eventually* . . . it was only three months ago!"

"I found *out* three months ago. By that time they'd split up anyway. Charles and I go back a long, long way, since kindergarten. I missed hanging out with him too much—forgive and forget and all."

141

"What if he does it again? With someone else?"

"He won't. He learned his lesson."

I wondered. Some friend. Cal seemed like such an easy-going person, too much so for his own good. "So? You never answered my question," I said, "where are your folks from?"

"I was avoiding your question because my story is pretty boring, my upbringing very run of the mill."

"Run of the mill is good. Means you're normal."

"So normal I'm dull."

"Actors are rarely dull. Too complex to be dull."

"Too egotistical you mean?"

"That too."

We both chuckled.

"I'm from Iowa."

"That's a long way from Hollywood. What got you into acting?"

"College play. Modeling got me a manager, and it went from there."

"I suspected you might have modeled."

"Suspected, Miss Marple?"

I laughed. "Your features are so . . . even, so perfect, I can see how you modeled."

"Yeah, well, I keep that side of things quiet, you know. Male models are kind of, I don't know . . . uninspiring."

"Oh, I think you'd inspire a lot of girls. And men."

"Thanks a lot, that's all I need. It was bad enough in college but now I get official fan mail from guys asking to date me."

"Where did you go to college?"

"MIT."

"No kidding? So you're some kind of rocket scientist?"

Cal laughed. "I was originally studying Nuclear Science and Engineering but then I transferred to Theater Arts after one year."

"You must be brainy to have been accepted at MIT in the first place."

"So they tell me. Your brain is only effective if you use it to full capacity, and I just wasn't a hundred percent committed to the program. They had an animal lab there for experiments. All I could think of was my dog back home and how it could be him, could have been Pepper in one of those cages. I switched courses."

"Yeah, I can totally identify with that. I had no idea Massachusetts Institute of Technology did arts courses though."

"Few people do. It was news to me as well. Anyway, I was a lot happier after I transferred. Dad wasn't so thrilled but hey, it's my life and it was what I wanted to do all along anyway. By the way, you hungry?"

"Actually, now that you mention it, Cal, I am. Felt so butterfly-ish earlier, I hardly ate lunch."

"I'll fix us something."

"How? Where?"

"Here, in this trailer."

"We have food?"

"Sure." Cal got up and rummaged through the kitchen cupboards. He threw a bag of chips at me. I tore them open—I was really hungry.

"I grabbed some fruit salad from the caterer earlier," he said. "Scored some yogurt—can make us some great smoothies."

My mouth was practically watering. "Wow, I'm impressed. I'm so lazy about food. I forget to eat and love readymade and takeout stuff, you know? Delicious, *gourmet* readymade; that's why I like living in New York City, I never have to think about cooking."

"I love to cook," Cal said, putting a banana and berries into a blender, navigating his way about the kitchenette like he lived here. He was so casual in everything he did, so confident, but without being cocky. The kind of guy you felt safe with, the kind who'd put up a tent or change your light bulb. Reliable. At least, that was the impression he was giving me. Maybe it was an act—like he said, he was an actor. But for now, I felt very at ease in his company.

"Well, cook away," I egged on, "I'll be your guest anytime. Apparently, back in the day, they didn't used to have catering on set like they do now. My mom told me that. Hard to imagine. Apparently they even brought their own sandwiches along in brown paper bags. When Liz Taylor was filming Cleopatra in Rome she got an urge for her favorite dish—chili from Chasen's—and had it flown over by jet."

Cal handed me my smoothie. "It would be fun to do stuff like that, wouldn't it? Behave outrageously, just because you had the means."

"Making some real money will be amazing,

that's for sure." I gulped down the tasty smoothie. "My God, this is delicious!" I was reluctant to talk too much about money though, in case Cal asked me how much they were paying me. I didn't want him to feel awkward if I was earning more than him, which I suspected I might be because of Cindy being such a Rottweiler.

"Is that what made you say yes to this movie, Janie? The money? Cause I'd have thought for a successful theater actress like you this kind of job was a little risqué."

"Oh, you know, it just kind of happened. I said no, but then I ended up saying yes. Bills, a huge student loan to pay back, curiosity, and a chance I may never get again."

"Do you wish Daniel Glass was still on board?" Cal's gaze lingered on me as if he were searching into my soul.

I answered quickly—too quickly perhaps—to sound casual. "Yes. And no. Yes because, as a director, I trust him a hundred percent. He gets the best out of his actors, always, even though he's tough, demanding and can seem like a real bastard sometimes, but he knows what he's doing. He's an actor's director. He used to be an actor at the beginning of his career so he totally *gets* actors, you know? He treats a person with a walk-on part the same as a big star."

"He was an actor? I didn't know that."

"Mostly theater. Apparently he was really talented, but he started writing and directing plays so stopped acting."

"And the 'no' part?"

"Excuse me?"

"You said, 'yes' you were glad he was no longer involved in this film and 'no.' Why no?"

I thought about it for a second. Cal's question was too direct to be comfortable. The truth was I had no satisfactory answer. "He's so intense he . . . he gets under your skin."

"You really into him or something?"

I laughed, probably too falsely. "No way! It's just people want to please him too much. He has that effect on everyone who works with him. Actors become obsessed with . . . with, I don't know, *competing* with one another to be Daniel's protégée, to be the favorite."

"Were *you* his favorite?"

"No, I never was. He was tougher on me than the rest of the cast."

"But you got a Tony nomination."

"Hey! You said you hadn't done the full stalk on me."

"If I'd done the full stalk I would have known you were from Vermont."

There was a knock at the door. "Yeah?" Cal called out.

A face peered in. "Miss Cole, and Mr. Haplan, you're needed on set."

"You're Maggie, aren't you?" I asked. The girl was a little younger than me. Wide-eyed, and with a lot of excess nervous energy—she was drumming her fingers on the door. I remembered Star's tip of getting to know everybody's names and making friends. "By the way, please call me by my first name—call me Janie, 'Miss' sounds so weird."

Cal got up. "Me too, call me Cal."

"Cool," she said. "Makeup is waiting on set for a touch-up. Better hurry."

I glanced in the mirror. I was already caked in makeup and wondered how they could possibly slap on more. The makeup artist assured me I looked "natural", but seeing my reflection reminded me of a dry, sun-bleached riverbed, with cracks in it. Powder, to stop any shine on camera, kept getting applied and reapplied as false alarms of going for a take made them rush at us with brushes and little sponges. The lipstick would be out in full force too, because of the smoothie wiping half of it off. Making a movie was so much less glamorous than I had imagined.

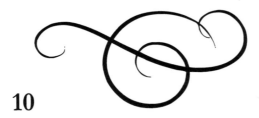

10

WE WERE IN THE MIDDLE of shooting a scene in Jonathon's office. I was dressed in a tight gray pencil skirt and killer Louboutin heels. Movies are shot out of sequence and this was well after our characters had met, somewhere midway in the script. The director had me leaning against the desk, the edge of my butt perched there seductively. I had to smooth my hands along the front of my skirt while the camera came in close, as it panned down Jonathon's fingers unbuttoning my blouse and hooking into my waistband, at which point Simon would yell "cut." We did this several times.

Take five and it still wasn't perfect. The makeup on my cheeks felt crusty and old and my face wasn't even in shot. Just my torso. My hands were trembling. Ridiculous. *Not* acting was far harder than acting. I didn't even have a line to say. Daniel had been right. All this (me) would be larger than life on screen. I felt aware of my bra peeking through my top. Cal had to brush his fingers slowly around my front, softly caressing my cleavage. Meanwhile, six people surrounded us with cameras, booms, bounce boards, and God knows what else. There was my makeup artist, a brush poised in one eager hand. More powder? *You cannot be serious!*

While they were fiddling about with the lights, my mind wandered winsomely back to my stage career. I felt homesick. Cal, sensing my unrest, touched my hand, but then it was whisked away by Sandra, my makeup artist. She inspected my manicured nails. Manicured in neat French polish by her, at dawn this morning.

"They're okay," she confirmed, "nails are looking good."

"It gets better," Cal assured me in a whisper.

"When?"

"When we get to the meaty scenes with more dialogue. You'll see."

Hours and hours, all day, for two minutes' screen time. I yawned, quickly covering my boredom with my entire arm to try and hide my exhaustion. Exhaustion from doing nothing since six o'clock this morning.

"Quiet on set please, going for a take," the director yelled. "You ready, Janie?" He pinned his glare on me.

"Never readier," I said, giving him a honeyed grin.

"Camera rolling."

"And . . . action!"

I smoothed my skirt. It had to be just so. Too far to the left or right and my hand would be out of shot. Cal started with his movements. His fingers brushed tenderly up my waist and, being ticklish in that particular spot, I started giggling. Uncontrollably. My body was shaking . . . trembling. I looked at Cal and a new rush of silent hysteria caused my body to quiver anew. His subtle smile didn't give way to laughter like me—he remained calm, professional.

"And cut!" Simon shouted. "Janie, are you okay?"

"I'm fine." And I burst out laughing again like

some crazed hyena.

THE PRODUCERS WATCHED the dailies and decided that my trembling body looked great. Because we didn't have any lines, it would be easy for them to dub over with music and sound effects. However, my unprofessionalism did not go unnoticed by the director. Tension was in the air, which only made me want to laugh even more. Like being at class in school. I managed to hold it in, but the director was watching me with a stern, sharp eye.

The next scene we had to shoot was our first kiss. I decided to really go for it. Cal was gorgeous and sexy and as sweet as could be—I couldn't have been luckier. The scene was taking place in the back of a limo. The limo—which had been adapted especially for the shot—was even bigger than a real life limo. I was topless, wearing little nipple covers called pasties. The shot would only show my shoulders and be cut just above my breasts. All very technical but it was in my no nudity clause. Cal had to pretend he was sucking my tits. There was to be a hard close up on his mouth as the camera followed his trail from my bellybutton up, a cut to a close-up of my rapturous face, then back to Cal's tongue traveling up my shoulders and neck to our mouths.

I didn't even know where we were in the script; half of it made no sense to me anyway. The storyline was all over the place. Jonathon was pretty psychotic; one minute loving, the next shunning me. My character was a wimp—I'd have told this Jonathon character to fuck right off a long time ago. But Simon didn't want us straying from the script even by one word. A far cry from how Daniel had envisioned us ad-libbing and improvising.

I got into position, stretched out on the limo's back seat. The lights were so glaring I couldn't see a thing, just felt hot. Two cameras were pointed into the limo. Cal was on his knees, his body twisted at an angle. Very unnatural, but apparently it looked great through the lens.

"And . . . action!" Simon boomed.

"You. Are. So. Hot. Baby," Cal panted, tracing his tongue around my navel and clinching my waist with his large hands, careful not to set off my ticklish spot.

I don't know what came over me but I gritted between my teeth, "I'm not your baby, Jonathon."

"Cut!" cried Simon. "Janie, what the hell! That's not your line!"

"I don't have any lines in this scene, Simon."

"Exactly! So what are you doing?"

"Trying to bring some life force into my character. She's so—"

"Submissive?"

"Yes."

"She's *meant* to be submissive, Janie. That's the whole *point!*"

"There's submissive and there's boring," I quipped.

"Just do your goddamn job please, so we can all go home."

I found myself rolling my eyes like a wayward teenager but then quickly pretended I had a stray eyelash so I didn't appear like I had an attitude. "Fine, I'm sorry, it won't happen again."

"Quiet on set please, going for a take!" the AD

called out. "Camera ready? Sound ready?"

"Ready."

"Camera rolling."

"Take two, scene thirty-one."

"And . . . action!"

Cal started his stuff again. I should have felt turned on in some way, but I wasn't. Not Cal's fault at all. I squirmed in the seat and started pretend groaning and biting my lower lip. This was not what I trained at Juilliard for; my mother would be rolling in her grave. I writhed around like a porn star, remembering the scale of my debts, knowing I had to shut my smart mouth and just get on with it. I moaned again and flexed my hips up toward Cal. In my peripheral vision I saw he had a boner.

Well, at least one of us was into this.

We took a short break and Cal said in a low voice so only I could hear, "You know, Janie, if this were Woody Allen you might get fired."

"Even though we've already shot so much footage? It would be too expensive to fire me now."

"Woody sometimes fires actors almost midway through the shoot, if he thinks the actor isn't right for the part."

"Oh."

Cal went on, "They do mid-shoot replacements all the time. Harvey Keitel had already started filming *Apocalypse Now*, but got fired and was replaced by Martin Sheen."

"Providential, really—it wouldn't have been the same without Martin Sheen."

"Apparently Harvey had an attitude."

Like me. "Oh," I said again. I thought of Daniel once comparing me to Kate from Shakespeare's *Taming of the Shrew*. He didn't mind it when I challenged him though—when it had to do with work, anyway. He thought it was healthy for actors to have opinions and questions. But I knew that a lot of other directors, with less confidence in themselves, would interpret it as cocky or arrogant. Like Simon.

Cal went on, "One of the most famous firings in movie history was Eric Stoltz—you remember him? He was originally set to play Marty McFly in

Back to the Future. They'd even filmed forty whole minutes screen time with him, but they decided he was too serious for a comedy."

"Wow, Cal, I didn't know you were such a movie nerd. And I also didn't know that kind of thing happened, at least not to that extent." *How naïve could I be?* I could just see that was where I was headed. So much for my fleeting film career!

"You're doing great though," he said, "don't worry about it."

The truth was, I *wasn't* that worried. I mean, I was—I wanted to do a great job and not be the laughing stock of Hollywood, but I also felt deceived by this business. Everything felt so mechanical, so inorganic. The director treated us like puppets and paid far more attention to the lighting, or if my hair or something was shadowing my face, than the acting. The takes were short, which meant the editors would have a lot of work to do. It was hard to get into the flow of it. Filming felt like a game of American football. Stop, start, stop, start. I didn't feel as if I were offering anything except my body and my face—I wasn't being nourished as an actor. As an artist.

I now wished Daniel hadn't abandoned the project. It would have been different with him. Artistic. Creative.

Damn Daniel Glass. Why couldn't I rid him from my thoughts? He invaded every part of me, even when I was working.

Especially when I was working.

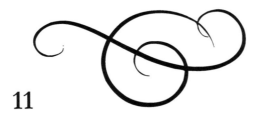

11

THE NEXT DAY, I was summoned by Samuel Myers himself. I knew what would happen next: I'd be unceremoniously fired. They probably had the contract so air tight that I had compromised something somewhere and wouldn't get all my fee. And who was I to try and sue? A nobody. Just a little, itty-bitty actress in the big greasy wheel that was Hollywood. I'd go back to my moldy apartment and start auditioning for plays again. Maybe I'd even need to beg for my old waitressing job back, although I doubted they'd take me. I'd been foolish. Not grateful enough. And now I was going to get my comeuppance.

I had one hour before I needed to leave for our "meeting" . . . the *firing*. I sat on the living room floor, playing Barbies with Hero. Star was in the kitchen with Jake, both making lunch. They did things like that; cooked meals together. I wondered if that would ever be me. Maybe Cal would be up for making meals with me, although in my fantasies he'd do all the cooking.

"This is my Computer Engineer Barbie," Hero told me, holding up the blond bombshell doll, who was wearing pink plastic glasses. Hero was a strong little thing, all of six and a half years old, already a veteran movie star. She knew all about hitting her mark, camera angles, even which side of her face looked best. "This is my naughty side," she had told me last week, pointing to the left side of her face, "and this is the cute side."

"Oh yeah? And which side gets the ice cream?" I asked.

"The cute side, for sure." She blinked her long lashes at me, and swept a hand through her Shirley Temple curls. Scary. She knew the power she had already, especially when it came to her doting dad.

She now sat cross-legged on the floor, arranging her dolls and teddies, her lips pursed in concentration. We were making a school.

"I heard all about this Computer Barbie," I

said. "Apparently she gets the boys to fix her computer and doesn't do those kinds of things for herself." I thought of myself, letting anyone, and everyone, cook for me. A real live Blanche Dubois.

Hero fiddled with her doll's synthetic golden hair. "Oh, she knows how to fix her computer. She knows *a lot*. She just asks the boys because she's too busy."

I grinned although Hero's serious face made me bite my tongue. "Oh yeah? What's she busy doing?"

"She runs her own company, of course. She can't do *everything* herself, she has boys working for her."

"I like your take on that, Hero. Very interesting. Very astute."

"What's astoot?"

"It means that your Barbie is a lot cleverer than people give her credit for," said her mom. Star was standing at the doorway, watching us. "Never underestimate a pretty face. When she gets guys to do stuff for her, she has a reason. Lunch is on the table." She clapped her hands. "And . . . action!"

Like mother, like daughter, I thought with a

smile.

CAL CAME TO PICK ME UP in his Mustang convertible. He insisted that I didn't go to the meeting alone. Not that he'd be coming in with me, but at least he'd be there, waiting for me when I came out (probably in floods of tears), realizing what an idiot I'd been to bungle up my one big chance.

"Everything happens for a reason," he said in a gentle voice, as he drove out of Star and Jake's driveway.

"That's such a cliché," I mumbled.

"Clichés are clichés because they're nearly always true."

"I have a sixty thousand dollar student loan to pay off," I said. "Plus bills, rent et cetera. Why couldn't I have kept my big mouth shut?"

"Because you have a strong personality. You are who you are, Janie, you can't fight it."

"Simon hates me."

"No he doesn't, he's just under pressure to come in under budget."

I looked out the window at the view passing by. We were on Pacific Coast Highway, the ocean shimmering on our right, and palms taller than skyscrapers kissing the bright blue sky. New York would be cold and tough. I'd gotten used to luxury at Star's house, the warm breeze, the great views. I'd miss this. All because of my attitude. Oh well. Hollywood obviously wasn't my path in life.

Cal turned to me and squeezed my hand. "You're amazing, Janie. You're different."

"Different, like how?"

"Good different. Quirky. Kind of cocky, but vulnerable at the same time. Like you don't care but yet you do. I can't explain. But if they do let you go? Promise we can still hang out."

"Sure, I'd love that."

He shuffled in his seat. "You know, I have to admit after yesterday, after our sex scene in the limo, you kind of really *got* to me." He was silent for a beat and added, "I dreamt about you last night."

My smile tipped into a sardonic smirk. *Oh yeah, did I know all about dreams.* "A sexy dream?"

"*Very* sexy."

I noticed Cal had another stiffy straining through the fabric of his jeans. He spotted me eyeing his crotch.

"Shit, sorry, just thinking about my dream has gotten me all aroused again." He laughed. "I hope I'm not being crass."

"I'm flattered," I let him know.

"Janie, I kind of really tried to keep this professional between us, you know, getting involved during filming is not always the best idea in the world, but now . . . "

"I'm going to be fired?"

"Hey, we don't know that for sure."

"I think we do. You saw Simon whispering to George yesterday. He's fed up with me. It's so over for me."

"Janie, I'd like to take you out. Get to know you better, off set. I thought we could maybe go for a little road trip or something? Go up PCH? Santa Barbara? Get away for a couple of days."

Cal was such a gentleman. Not only had he opened my car door for me but was asking my permission to date me. The old fashioned way. He was salt-of-the-earth. A nice, mid western boy with manners and morals. I'd been so wrapped up with my Daniel obsession that I hadn't given anyone else a chance. Mainly because I hadn't met some-one I'd found attractive in New York, amongst the plethora of gay guys and short actors with chips on their shoulders. Cal was different. A breath of fresh air.

I laid my hand on his muscly thigh. His erection stood back to attention the second I touched him. A good sign if ever there was one. I was sick of the unrequited love bullshit. Not once had Daniel ever hinted at asking me out after his wife died. Not even for a coffee. And kissing me, when I was offering myself up so wantonly like fruit on a platter, did *not* count.

"You know what, Cal? I'd love that."

He heaved out a heavy sigh—he'd been holding his breath, waiting for my answer.

Finally I'd found a man who was real *boyfriend* material. Not some OCD perfectionist freak like Daniel, who was in love with another woman anyway—even still—and would be for years to come.

"You know what, Cal?" I said again, squeezing his firm leg. "You're a really cool person." I looked at his handsome face. Damn, he was fine. His mop of dark hair hung heavy over his brow and his beautiful brown eyes—rimmed with shockingly thick eyelashes—glimmered with hope.

He opened his mouth to say something but he stopped himself. But I knew a guy in love when I saw one—and Cal was falling for me. Hard.

Hard, in more ways than one.

And it pleased me to have him so into me.

But the real question was . . .

Would I be able to get Daniel out of my system?

I TIPTOED INTO Samuel Myers's office in Century City, my sneakers making no sound as I slipped through the door. He was expecting me; his PA had just called him, but when I peered my head into the room I thought at first it was empty. Music was playing softly. Something classical. I looked around. Nobody was here. The room was vast and imposing, boasting floor to ceiling windows with skyline views. We were very high up— as high as you could be in LA for fear of earthquakes. A library lined one wall, replete with leather-bound books. Grand sofas and armchairs sprawled themselves on one side, and on the other there was a bar. In the middle, a massive conference table.

I suddenly had an uneasy feeling in my gut.

Samuel hadn't called me in here to fire me. No! He had other plans: to seduce me. My mind wandered back to my mother, the "being chased around the casting couch" story, with the "repulsive, gold medallioned director." Samuel Myers scored no higher in the beauty stakes. He'd called me in to woo me. Or worse, blackmail me. "Give me a blowjob or you're off the movie." Ugh!! Gross.

Because where the hell was he? This was no bona fide "meeting!" I had imagined that Pearl Chevalier would be here too, and maybe one of the executive producers—a room full of them ready to offer their condolences, yet firing me simultaneously, paradoxically sugary-sweet smiles on their faces.

"Hello?" I called out tentatively. "Mr. Myers?"

A deep voice rumbled from somewhere in the library. "Hi, Janie. They just stepped out. They'll be back in a minute."

Goose bumps spread across my flesh. What the fuck was *he* doing here?

"Daniel?" I couldn't see him, but I knew that unmistakable voice. I detected the sound of pages being turned, mingled with the gentle melody of the classical music playing in the background.

Then Daniel spoke again, his deep, theatrically trained voice resonating:

> *"Hope is the thing with feathers*
> *That perches in the soul,*
> *And sings the tune without the words,*
> *And never stops at all.*
>
> *And sweetest in the gale is heard;*
> *And sore must be the storm*
> *That could abash the little bird*
> *That kept so many warm.*
>
> *I've heard it in the chilliest land*
> *And on the strangest sea;*
> *Yet, never, in extremity,*
> *It asked a crumb of me."*

I stood there, motionless, my limbs floating—at least it felt that way. The words of that beautiful poem brought back a memory that I couldn't place.

"Emily Dickinson," I murmured to myself, "I love that poem." I noiselessly walked over to the library and saw Daniel, not on one of the sofas, but on the floor, books spread about him, his head cast downwards, as he thumbed through an old leather-bound volume. Why *that* particular poem? Was it random? *Hope is the thing with feathers.* Did he mean *me*? That *I* was hoping? Hoping for a real relationship with him? The little bird that didn't ask for even a crumb? Because it was true; I had never asked anything of Daniel, but I had *hoped.* Hopelessly hoped. I shook myself out of my reverie and back to the point in question . . .what was Daniel goddamn Glass *doing* here, anyway?

He said nothing, just continued to thumb through the book. He didn't even turn to look at me, so absorbed as he was. I wondered if he could sense my presence. Finally he raised his head.

"Do you always slink up on people that way?" he said wryly. I had forgotten how much his eyes affected me. Just a glance was all it took. My stomach somersaulted on itself.

"Do you always gatecrash my meetings?" I retorted, a faint smile sneaking on my lips.

"I was invited here."

He was wearing a blue T-shirt that accentuated his pectorals and the color of his eyes, and a pair of worn jeans. All I could think of was the delicious package tucked away inside, and a flash of one of my sexy dreams replayed in my brain.

"Janie! You got here!" It was Sam Myers bursting through a side door, with Pearl Chevalier in tow.

Daniel gathered the books together and put them on the coffee table in front of him. He turned and said, "Damn, I was hoping to have a moment alone with you, Janie."

Samuel thundered into the room, donned in a cream-colored suit that was too tight for him. Beads of sweat glittered on his forehead. I was tempted to hotline a call to my makeup artist to take away the shine. He was smiling inanely. This whole situation was confusing to say the least.

"Janie, so glad you could come," Pearl said, offering me her cheek. Her skin was perfect—smooth and flawless. She really was beautiful and very un-LA, sophisticated, dressed in nude high heels and a navy blue suit. Another man came into the room, seconds later. One of the producers? He was debonair. Tall, dark, and unbelievably handsome. Not dissimilar to Daniel; an unusual, original face, but with green eyes, not blue—equally piercing, though.

"Janie, so 'appy to mit you," he said, his

French accent taking me by surprise. I realized it was Pearl's husband, the billionaire owner of Hooked Up, Alexandre Chevalier. He shook my hand. All three of them were beaming at me. I glanced over at Daniel, and he winked, his lip slipping into an ironic curve, which suggested amusement. *What the hell was going on?*

"Who'd like a drink?" Samuel exclaimed with a hearty wheeze. "Champagne, anyone?" He made his way to the bar and took out a bottle of Bollinger from the icebox. "Pearl, honey, would you get some glasses? You know where they are."

"We don't want to jump the gun," Daniel warned.

"Oh, I think we have cause for celebration," Samuel snorted.

"Well, Janie, I just wanted to say hi," Alexandre said, kissing my hand with a flourish, "welcome aboard The Enterprise, and see you around." He turned on his heel and strode out the door.

Samuel puffed out his large belly. I thought his suit buttons would pop. "Take a seat, Janie, make yourself comfortable. Daniel, explain to our Rambling Rose, here, what's going on."

I made my way over to the library, Daniel meeting me halfway. To my surprise he kissed me on the cheek, while his hand slid over my hip. "Missed you, Janie," he whispered in my ear. Then he stood back when he noticed my bewildered expression. "What, did you think they'd asked you here to fire you?" He knew me so well.

"No," I lied, "of course not."

"Like hell," he said.

"Why am I here, then?"

"Ah, you said, 'then' . . . so you *did* think you'd be fired."

"Who thinks they'll be fired?" Samuel roared. "Oh, him. He doesn't know it yet."

Doesn't know it yet? Who doesn't know it yet? This was becoming more mysterious by the minute.

Pearl brought a tray of glasses over and set them on the coffee table. Samuel popped open the bottle of champagne and poured. I slumped on the sumptuous sofa, and Daniel sat next to me. Pearl perched herself on the edge of an armchair and Samuel remained standing.

"Janie, we've been watching the dailies and everybody is very happy with your performance," Samuel said.

"More than happy," Pearl added.

I covered my hands over my eyes and let out a long sigh.

"What's wrong?" Samuel asked.

I uncovered my relieved face. "Nothing, just wondered what this meeting was all about," I answered, "wondered if you were dissatisfied in some way."

Samuel handed me a flute of champagne. "I'll cut to the chase. Simon's gotta go."

"But so much is in the can already," I pointed out. 'In the can,' meaning already shot—I was beginning to sound like a pro. "Everyone's been talking about coming in under budget, we—"

"I'm coming back on board," Daniel interrupted. "With full artistic license to shoot the film how I envision."

My heart was pounding—so much information. "Which is?"

"The sex scenes in black and white, which gives me leeway to be more . . . more creative, more experimental."

"More experimental?"

"Would you be willing to be filmed nude?" Pearl asked me. "In other words, your nudity clause, Janie, would be null and void. Daniel would need the freedom to shoot at his own discretion. That would need complete trust on your part."

I sat there, speechless.

"You'd have a closed set, of course," Pearl added, "a privacy patch et cetera—I'm sure costume has explained all this to you and—"

"Janie, it's in my interest, and in the producers' interest, to make you look good," Daniel interrupted, "and . . . what's the right word . . . classy."

I took a sip of champagne, thinking of the "privacy patch", a skimpy bit of flesh-colored fabric that would barely cover my hoo-ha. No toast had been made and people had already started drinking, as if it was a done deal. "I don't understand. I mean, Mr. Myers, what made you have a change of heart? I thought you and Daniel disagreed on the look and feel of the movie, and that's why he pulled out."

"Firstly, Janie, call me Sam. And secondly, in my line of business it's important to recognize when you're wrong. I misjudged you—which I was happy to admit—and I misjudged the *project*. I had originally wanted *The Dark Edge of Love* to be a blockbuster, to compete side by side with *Fifty*

Shades—"

"Which we all know is impossible," Pearl cut in. "Not only do they have an immense budget, but an unlimited fan base, impossible to compete with. That's why we came to the conclusion our movie needs to go in the opposite direction and return to Daniel's original concept. Artistic, with a European feel to it. Sam is the first to admit he got sidetracked, but he's a hundred percent with us now."

I remembered Samuel Myers tax loss analogy. This mind changing would have cost them serious dollars. Maybe they didn't care. "Why does that go hand in hand with nudity?" I asked.

"It just does," Daniel said. "I can't be getting hung up over a right boob side shot or a centimeter too much of your ass."

"My ass?" The reality of it hit me. Black and white or not, my petite ass would be plastered across HD screens across the world, some of them, twenty feet high. My little tits, not lush melons, not even peaches, but tiny, unripe cherries. And my bony frame that, in my mind's eye, suddenly didn't seem like part of Star's sexy 'brand' packaging after all. "I don't know," I wavered. "I don't think I'm right for the part."

"You're the *only* one for the part," Daniel said, his tone emphatic. "I'm not interested in doing this project without you, Janie. As I said, I want a theatrically trained actress, someone who can improvise, someone who can sustain one, long, fifteen minute take."

"What about a body double?" I offered, suspecting Daniel wouldn't go for it.

"Defeats the purpose. This film is about acting, about passion and love, not about body parts. I can't be spending more time faffing about in the editing room than on set."

"What about Cal?" I asked. "Will he be shooting nude too?" I'd heard about what actors had to wear: a "cock-sock" to cover up their private parts. I tried to picture Cal in a cock-sock, getting an erection and it springing off like a slingshot.

Daniel cleared his throat as if he were about to speak but then stayed silent. He looked at Samuel.

"Look," Sam said, "the truth is, and the truth can hurt sometimes . . . it's like watching a wooden puppet and prima ballerina perform together. The wooden puppet is cute, but he's still made of wood. The prima ballerina is flesh and blood, she's alive—you know what I'm saying?"

"Who's the puppet and who's the ballerina?" I asked. I had a good idea but wanted to hear it from his lips.

"Cal," Daniel said, his voice a hammer.

Pearl smoothed her pencil skirt over her fine legs. She wasn't wearing pantyhose—she didn't need them. "Look," she began, "Cal is very, very handsome, and for a soap or light comedy he's perfect, but seeing you together just . . . just . . . it's like oil and water, it isn't working."

"It's not his fault!" I blurted out. "We've had zero direction from Simon. Cal is a good actor, he just needs direction!"

Daniel shot me a look, which I couldn't read.

"Cal's gotta go too," Samuel stated without remorse. "He'll get his full fee, don't feel badly for the boy."

A chill spiraled through my limbs. Cal would be devastated. I felt somehow that it was my fault, that I was responsible. Had I upstaged him? Had I unwittingly made him look bad? "He's a good actor," I repeated. "He's professional, reliable, he's a nice guy!"

"We don't give a damn about nice," Sam

hurled out. "We want menacing, we want danger-ous."

"We need drop-dead sexy, not just good look-ing," Pearl added. "I did ask my husband if he wanted the role, but . . ." —she winked at me— "but we've gone down another avenue."

"Another avenue?" I echoed, my heart still pounding at the thought of stripping naked in front of Daniel, directing me to do anything he wanted, to have 'artistic control' over my body— considering he pretty much already owned my mind. "What actors have you considered?"

"Just one actor," Pearl said, looking at Daniel as if for his approval. I'd heard the name of Bran-don Taylor being bandied about, the latest hotshot movie star who everyone was raving about. Per-haps they'd choose him to replace Cal.

Sam took a long gulp of champagne. "We've decided he would be the best thing for the movie."

"Who?" I asked.

"Me," Daniel rumbled. "I'm going to be your leading man, your co-star. I'm a trained actor, might as well put my skills to use. Yes or no, Janie? You need to decide."

I sat there, silent, gob-smacked by the humdinger news. Had I heard this right? Not only was Daniel Glass going to now direct *The Dark Edge of Love* but he was also going to REPLACE CAL AS MY LEADING MAN! I could feel my limbs trembling. Not tickle induced laughter this time, no, but terror. And I had been doing so well! I thought of Cal, waiting for me, planning a weekend away. Of how relieved I was, just an hour ago, to be mentally free of Daniel—to be getting on with my life, moving forward.

And now look.

"I don't know," I said in a quiet voice. Samuel, Pearl, and Daniel were waiting, their gazes fixed to me for a concrete answer: was I going to bare all in this movie? Strip myself of my nicely worked out nudity clause that had been gone over with a fine toothcomb by one of Hollywood's finest entertainment lawyers? Strip myself in every way.

Samuel's voice was a cleaver to my rumination. "Look, Janie, I like you. We can up your fee. Not by a lot but—"

"It's not the money," I broke in.

"Sam, Janie doesn't have to decide this very second!" Pearl said. "Let's finish our drinks and take a rain check."

"What about Cal?" I asked.

"Cal will be just fine," Samuel said.

Any second now I would see Cal. There was no way I could look him in the face, knowing what I knew, and not share it with him. I was disgusted by their cavalier attitude. They all had immense wealth and stellar careers. Amazing how people with everything forget what it's like for the rest of us who have to fight for our chances. And the money wasn't the whole of it; this part was a big break for Cal—for any actor. Losing it would be devastating even if he did still get his paycheck.

"He's waiting for me," I let them know.

Pearl glared at Samuel. "I told you we should have talked to Cal first," she whispered.

Samuel threw up his arms in the air. Or tried. His tight suit jacket restrained him. "We don't even have an answer from Janie yet, how could we have spoken to Cal first?"

Daniel turned abruptly to me. "Cal's *waiting* for you? What? *Here?*"

"Yes, he's just outside the door." A look of perplexity swept across the director's face. "We're seeing each other," I added. The words flew out of my mouth. Maybe I wanted to punish Daniel in some way. Let him know he didn't own me. No, I had other options; men who weren't still living in the past, and using women for sex to make themselves feel better. Men who weren't control freaks. It was crazy that Daniel would be playing the lead of Jonathon, even though I knew several actor/directors had had huge success wearing both hats: Robert Redford, Sean Penn—the list went on. But still, Daniel taking control in this way unnerved me. I had already sublet my apartment— I couldn't go back to New York right now anyway. I had made a commitment to the bank to pay off my sixty thousand dollar student loan. Saying 'no' to *The Dark Edge of Love* would turn my life upside down.

But if I said 'yes' my life would *still* be turned upside down. In a different way.

Pearl got up. "Well, I'm going to ask Cal to come inside and we can talk this over. I'm very happy to offer extra severance pay, from my own pocket if need be. None of this is his fault." She walked toward the door.

I didn't care to see Cal's disappointed face when he found out the bad news, so I excused myself to use the bathroom. I guess that was cowardly, but there it was.

I stayed in there as long as possible. I heard low voices, muttering, no expletives or anything, just benign murmuring, like white noise. I splashed cold water on my face, and when I went to use the toilet, blood in my panties made me realize that all this stress had brought on my period a week early. That happened sometimes when I was stressed— my period might last a day only. And I was sure feeling stressed now. Was it always like this, this thankless, feckless film business? Or was it only Hollywood? Actors being exchanged like commodities without any thought for how that person in question would actually *feel*? No wonder actors became demanding when they got to be famous. Their way of saying "I won't take this shit anymore! Finally you can treat me like a human being."

I rummaged about in my purse and luckily found a tampon. Washed my hands, found some French hand cream and, after several minutes killing time, stood with my scented, moisturized hand on the doorknob, braving myself to return. I still hadn't made up my mind.

I needed more time.

I tentatively turned the door handle. Daniel was right there, in the corridor between the bathroom and Samuel's office, his face suddenly in my face, his blue *blue* eyes windows, not to *his* soul, but to *mine*. They undid me every single time. Left me open, vulnerable, and weak. Lightheaded. My heart racing out of sequence.

"Janie." He pinned me against the wall, his gaze raking me up and down. He stroked my cheek with his thumb, letting it linger along the edge of my jaw. "Please say yes."

"Daniel, I—"

"I need you, Janie."

"Your wife would have been perfect for this role, but not me," I fired out, and immediately wished I hadn't opened my mouth. I sounded bitter, bitchy and jealous. Which of course, I was. Jealous of a dead woman. *Get a life, Janie!*

"If only you knew." One side of his mouth lifted at the corner sardonically.

"If only *you* knew how you're doing my head in!" I shot back. "How do you think this is for me? Yes, no, yes, no. Finally I'd gotten the swing of things with Cal, and boom! You're back in the picture!"

"This is all about Cal?" he asked, incredulously. "*Cal?*"

"What just happened now? In there while I was in the bathroom?"

"He was let go."

"Why don't people tell it how it is? He wasn't 'let go,' he was unceremoniously fired!"

"He's fine, Janie, believe me. If that film had been made in the direction it was going, it would have ruined his career. And yours. I saw the dailies. It was a pile of shite."

"A pile of shite?"

"The Irish have a poetic way of saying things and yes, it was a pile of fucking *shite*."

I couldn't help but smile. But my heart was pounding through my chest and out the other side having Daniel so close. He knew exactly what he was doing. Using me. Using me to get what he wanted. He knew I was obsessed with him, it was written all over my face, in every breath I took. He wanted me as his little marionette to dance to his tune while he waltzed about Hollywood, or whatever capital he happened to be in, shagging Natasha Jürgen lookalikes. I'd heard more on that front. Jake had heard rumors too about the Daniel

Glass Shagathon.

"So you're my knight in shining armor coming on his galloping steed to rescue me from this 'pile of shite?' " I said, sarcastically.

Daniel ran his tongue along his lower lip then nipped it between his teeth. "That's right, I'm your knight in shining armor. You'll look beautiful the way I'm going to shoot you. Long languid takes, black and white for the sex scenes but with maybe a dash of color. Red. On your lips. Or red panties. Or a lone red rose in a vase. The color can be added later in post-production. Grainy black and white. Low lighting. Slow mo. You'll look fucking amazing. A class act. What do you say?"

"Why? Why did you change your mind?"

"You really want to know?"

"Yes, I do."

"Because I heard they were making a fucking meal of it and I couldn't stand to see your career go down the toilet."

I digested what he said. Still, it wasn't enough of an explanation. "Why *you* as the actor? There are lots of great theater actors you could choose from for the role of Jonathon. Why *you*?"

"He's not called Jonathon any more. The character's named Finn now."

"The improvisation has started already, has it?" My tone was sarcastic.

"You bet." He leaned in closer and let his lips brush lightly against mine. *Oh God.* "We can start improvising right now," he murmured into my mouth.

"Why you?" My echo was a whisper, I could hardly breathe—he'd sucked the air clean out of my lungs with his proximity.

His blue eyes seared into me. "Because I don't want any other man fucking touching you."

It took several seconds for me to process his words. Professional jealousy? I could feel my heart swell. Not in a good way but in an I'm-going-to-have-a-coronary sort of way. But I wouldn't let him get off so easily and manipulate me with a click of his finger as he was so used to doing. I wanted him to *feel.* To *hurt.*

"Well I'm seeing Cal. We've started dating," I half lied.

His eyes turned dark, a flash of fury, and it pleased me to no end. I felt lightheaded and dizzy even. *Let him experience the stab. Let him know what it's like to think about me having sex with someone else, the way I have envisioned him fucking all these busty blondes.*

"There'll be no dating Cal," he stated, as if it were a fact.

I raised my brows, haughtily. "Oh no? What makes you so sure?"

"Because he's getting on a plane in an hour. I'm having a car take him to Van Nuys, where he'll catch one of my jets to New York."

"One of your jets?"

He flicked his wrist in a dismissive wave as if his wealth was of no importance. "My father had an automobile parts empire. I still have shares in his company, and every now and again I take advantage of the perks it has to offer."

"So you're putting Cal on a jet? Why? So he can't get in the way of filming? So I won't be able to concentrate on anyone but you so you can control me like malleable putty for your work of art?" I was out of breath, my tirade a torrent.

Daniel gripped my wrists. "Janie, why are you so blind? So stubborn? Isn't it crystal clear?"

"It's as clear as *glass*. I know who you are, Daniel *Glass*! You're a megalomaniac who wants everyone to tow the line. You don't want me for *me*, you want me so that I can make you shine.

Polish your ego 'til it gleams! Be your little star student actress while you nurse your . . . your . . ."

I wanted to say 'blonde bimbo addiction' but I stopped myself. His wife was blond and I sounded like a psycho talking ill of the dead. Besides, she'd been anything *but* a bimbo. Anything but. I actually put my hand over my mouth so I didn't make a total jealous bitchy fool out of myself.

Daniel's lips curled up: a lopsided smile that almost looked like a smirk. He seemed not only amused, but pleased by my outburst.

"Janie, Janie, Janie. My little Janie Juilliard. Such a feisty little Kate, aren't we? Claws out, ready to fight and scratch. Such a wild shrew! Am I going to have to *tame* you? Whip you into shape? Take you over my knee and spank you?" —then he whispered in my ear—"fuck some sense into you?"

I could hear myself cry out as my body went limp. I literally crumpled to the floor at the idea of Daniel spanking me and fucking me. Had I heard him right?

Maybe not, because the next thing I knew, I blacked out.

TO BE CONTINUED . . . .

Book Two, **Broken Glass,** will be released soon.

Thank you so much for choosing **Shards of Glass** to be part of your library and I hope you enjoyed reading it as much as I enjoyed writing it. If you loved this book and have a minute please write a quick review. It helps authors so much. I am thrilled that you chose my book to be part of your busy life and hope to be re-invited to your bookshelf with my next release.

If you haven't read my other books I would love you to give them a try. The Pearl Series is a set of five, full-length erotic romance novels. If you'd like to know more about Star and Jake, you can read their story in *The Star Trilogy*. I have also written a suspense novel, *Stolen Grace.*

The Pearl Trilogy
(all three books in one big volume)

Shades of Pearl
Shadows of Pearl
Shimmers of Pearl
Pearl
Belle Pearl

The Star Trilogy
Stolen Grace

Join me on Facebook
(facebook.com/AuthorArianneRichmonde)

Join me on Twitter
(@A_Richmonde)

For more information about me, visit my website
(www.ariannerichmonde.com).

If you would like to email me:
ariannerichmonde@gmail.com

Made in the USA
Lexington, KY
27 March 2015